伶牙俐齿 英语口语

商务篇

主编 何士军

编委 刘蒙之　沈亚英　刘金伟　何士军　陈　文
　　　　周　俭　贾礼国　李　煜　贺延情　张岳琢
　　　　赵俊锋　赵　雁　王晓东　李　琼　孙进涛
　　　　孙朝丽　米　祥

世界图书出版公司

西安 北京 广州 上海

图书在版编目(CIP)数据

伶牙俐齿英语口语·商务篇/何士军主编.—西安:世界图书
出版西安公司,2006.4
ISBN 7－5062－8083－3

Ⅰ.伶... Ⅱ.何... Ⅲ.英语—口语 Ⅳ.H319.9

中国版本图书馆 CIP 数据核字(2006)第 032361 号

伶牙俐齿英语口语·商务篇

主　　编	何士军	
责任编辑	陈宇彤	
视觉设计	吉人设计	

出版发行　世界图书出版西安公司
地　　址　西安市北大街 85 号
邮　　编　710003
电　　话　029－87653334　87653335(市场营销部)
　　　　　029－87653301(总编室)
传　　真　029－87653347
经　　销　全国各地新华书店
印　　刷　西安东江印务有限公司
开　　本　850×1168　1/32
印　　张　7.875
字　　数　120 千字

版　　次　2006 年 5 月第 1 版　2006 年 5 月第 1 次印刷
书　　号　ISBN 7－5062－8083－3/H·733
定　　价　12.00 元

前　言

　　为什么你不能缺少这本书？

　　如果说市面上的英语口语书多如牛毛，这是对的；如果再说这里面实际上真正好用的口语书并不多，这也没错。你知道如何挑选适合自己的口语书吗？标准有三：

　　一、内容实用，能想到七七八八的大事小事一个都不能少；

　　二、编排合理，也叫人性化，想查什么一翻就能翻到；

　　三、版式新颖，精心制作，便于查阅学习。

　　《伶牙俐齿英语口语》系列丛书就是在这些标准的指导下，推出的全新英语口语学习书。首先，它们虽然书小内容却不少，想读者所想，尽可能模拟所有相关场景的英语语句；句式多而不死板，学习者可根据需要随时替换其中的关键词，方便学习使用。其次，根据场景科学编排，不以琐碎为烦恼，慢工出细活，以关键词为目录，易查询。第三，制作精美，版式活泼，迎合读图时代的需要，使读者置身实际交流语境，在愉快的氛围下学习英语口语。

　　《伶牙俐齿英语口语》系列丛书内容涵盖生活、旅游、商务中各场景下的常用口语，并针对各场景，按照"基本句型"、"星级典句"、"回应方式"、"情景对话"以及"必备词汇"几个单元设计编排，方便记忆查询。

　　《伶牙俐齿英语口语》系列丛书分为生活篇、旅游篇和商务篇，学习者可根据需要自行选择。

编　者

2006 年 4 月

目　录

Chapter 1   Office Philosophy

Introduction 介绍

"大家好，我叫……，来自……，以后还要请大家多关照、多指教。"陌生人之间的隔阂其实只是一层窗户纸，是一点即透的。初次见面的自我介绍会很容易使你为大家所熟知并很快融入新的工作环境，而且你会给人留下随和、易相处的印象；或者你可以把你的新同事、新的商业伙伴介绍给其他的同事认识，这样会便于大家更好的交流沟通。

eHow 基本句型 Sentence Patterns

Hello, I'm Jane.

你好,我叫珍妮。

Hi! I don't think we've met. I'm Johnson Harris.

你好,我想我们还不认识。我叫哈里斯·约翰逊。

Hi! My name is John. Nice to meet you.

你好,我叫约翰。很高兴认识你。

May I introduce myself? I'm . . .

我可以自我介绍一下吗?我是……

If you don't mind, I'd like to introduce myself. I'm . . .

如果你不介意的话,我想介绍一下我自己,我是……

Allow me to introduce myself , I'm . . .

请允许我自我介绍一下,我是……

Hello, I'm . . . What's your name?

你好,我是……你叫什么?

May I take the liberty of introducing myself to you?

我可以冒昧地向你自我介绍吗?

——以上适合于自我介绍

John, this is Bob.

约翰,这是鲍勃。

Jane, do you know Bob?

珍妮,你认识鲍勃吗?

Mr. . . . , I'd like you to meet . . .

……先生,我想让你认识一下……

Allow/Let me to introduce . . .

请允许我介绍……

I would like you to meet . . .

我想让你见一下……

Let me introduce our new colleague . . .

让我介绍一下我们的新同事……

It is with great pleasure that I introduce to you. . .

我非常荣幸介绍你们认识……

——以上适合于向别人介绍你的新同事新朋友

Here is my card.

这是我的名片。

Please accept mine(business card).

请收下我的名片。

Thank you for your card.

谢谢你的名片。

I'd like you to have my business card.

请收下我的名片。

——以上适合于给予或者接受他人的名片

eHɪw 星级典句 ＼ Classical Sentences

You are Ted? I have often heard about you.

你是泰德？我经常听说你。

I'm very delighted to meet you.

很高兴认识您。

I think I have seen you some where.

我想我在哪里见过你。

If you need a tour of the city, we will be glad to help.

如果你想在城里转转，我们愿意效劳。

It's a great honor to know you.

认识你是我莫大的荣幸。

I'm honored to know you.

很荣幸认识你。

Where are you come from?

你来自哪里？

I'm very glad to have the opportunity to meet you.

很高兴有机会认识你。

 情景对话 Situational Dialogue

情景会话是最有效地学习地道英文的方式，看一看别人怎么说，想一想，我们自己和老外在同样的场景，我们也可以同样地脱口而出自然的英语。

Part 1

A: Hi! Allow me to introduce myself, I'm John.

B: Hi! I'm Jane. Nice to meet you.

A: Miss Jane? I have often heard about you.

B: Really? What have you heard?

A: Compliments and so on.

Part 2

A: Jane, I'd like you to meet John, he is our business fellow.

B: I'm very delighted to meet you, Mr. John. Here is my business
   card. (offers her business card first)

C: Nice to meet you, Miss Jane. Thank you for you card, and
   please accept mine. (offers his own card)

B: Is this your first time in Xi'an?

C: Yes. Pretty easy to tell, huh?

B: No, not really. We don't see many Americans.

C: Actually, I'm English.

B: Oh, well, if you need a tour of the city, we will be glad to help.

Part 3

A: It is with great pleasure that I introduce to you our new colleague John.

B: Oh, wait, sorry, please let me introduce myself.

A: OK, that is wonderful. Please!

B: Hello, I'm John, from Northwest University in Xi'an, I'm honoured here to work with you.

A: Furthermore, I want to make a complementarity. John is newcomer, so I hope everyone would help him as far as you can.

B: Thank you!

译文

Part 1

A: 你好,请允许我自我介绍一下,我叫约翰。

B: 你好,我叫珍妮。很高兴认识你。

A: 珍妮小姐? 我经常听说你。

B: 真的? 关于什么?

A: 都是赞扬之词。

Part 2

A: 珍妮,我想让你认识一下约翰,他是我们的生意伙伴。

B: 很高兴认识你,约翰先生。这是我的名片。(先递出名片)

C: 很高兴认识你,珍妮小姐。谢谢你的名片,也请收下我的。(递

上自己的名片）

B: 你是第一次来西安吗？

C: 是的。是不是很容易看出来？

B: 不，其实我们见到的美国人不多。

C: 事实上，我是英国人。

B: 哦，如果你想在城里转转，我们愿意效劳当导游。

Part 3

A: 我非常荣幸介绍你们认识我们的新同事约翰。

B: 哦，对不起请等一下。请允许我自我介绍一下。

A: 好的，那真是太好了。请！

B: 大家好，我叫约翰，毕业于西安的西北大学。非常荣幸能来到这和大家一起工作。

A: 此外，我想再做个补充。约翰是新来的，所以我希望大家都能够尽自己所能来帮助他。

B: 谢谢！

必备词汇　Necessary Vocabulary

introduce *v.* 介绍

complementarity *n.* 补充

newcomer *n.* 新到的人，新来的人

honoured *adj.* 荣幸的

business *n.* 生意，贸易，营业，买卖

fellow *n.* 伙伴

Praise 赞扬

　　用一句真心的赞扬的话来肯定同事的工作，不仅证明了你没有陷入盲目的嫉妒，而且还显示出你从容的胸襟。同事的努力得到你的认可，他的心也会怦然一动，你们之间的关系自然更加友善。

eHow 基本句型　Sentence Patterns

Well done!

干得好！

Excellent/Good work.

做得好。

You have been appointed . . .

你已经被任命为……

We all know you have done an excellent job.

我们都知道你的工作很出色。

You really did a good job.

工作干得不错。

Your effort to . . . is highly effective.

你在……方面的努力是卓有成效的。

eHow 星级典句　Classical Sentences

You flatter me.

您过奖了。

I have a long way to go yet.

我还需要努力。

You did an excellent job.

你工作得很出色。

Good job!

干得好！

Thank you for your hard work.

感谢你的努力工作。

I appreciate your effort very much.

我非常欣赏你为此做出的努力。

She got a promotion because she did a good job.

她因工作的出色而获得了提升。

I've always admired your work very much.

我一向很钦佩你的工作。

I've got to hand it to you, you really did a good job.

你真的表现很出色，我不得不称赞你。

You are one in a million!

你可真是百里挑一啊！

You are out of sight!

你好棒！

Your presentation is smashing.

你表现十分出色。

You are always so impressive.

你总是那么令人印象深刻。

eHｏw 回应方式　　Repartee

Thank you very much. I appreciate it.

谢谢。很感激您的赏赐。

It's nice of you to say so.

谢谢您这么说。

It's my pleasure.

很荣幸。

Thank you for saying so.

谢谢您这么说。

It's very kind of you to say so.

谢谢您这么说。

Appreciate.

非常感激。

eHw 情景对话 \ Situational Dialogue

Part 1

A: John, you have been appointed the new manager of the company.

B: I am fortune enough to get that position.

A: We all know you have done an excellent job. You deserve the promotion.

B: Thank you for saying so.

Part 2

A: John, your project made much profit for the company. You really did a good job.

B: You flatter me. If not having the support from our work team I couldn't have got the achievement.

A: Did they help you a lot?

B: Yes. We are efficient because of cooperation.

A: Done well. The company should put a premium on you in the form of bonus.

B: Thank you very much for saying so.

Part 3

A: John, you did an excellent work. Your effort to promote the profit of our company is highly effective.

B: It's my pleasure.

A: You are always so impressive. I've got to hand it to you, you really did a good job.

B: It's very kind of you to say so.

译文

Part 1

A: 约翰,你已经被任命为公司的经理了。

B: 我能得到那个职位真的很幸运。

A: 你的工作很出色,你应该得到提升的。

B: 谢谢您这么说。

Part 2

A: 约翰,你的项目给公司带来了巨大的利润。工作干得不错。

B: 您过奖了。如果没有来自团队的支持我不可能取得这样的成就。

A: 他们帮了你很多吗?

B: 是的,我们通过合作效率很高。

A: 做得好。公司应该以红利的形式来奖励你们。

A: 非常感谢您这么说。

Part 3

A: 约翰,工作干得很好啊。你为提升公司的利润而做出的努力是卓有成效的。

　B: 我很荣幸。

　A: 你总是那么令人印象深刻。你真的表现很出色,我不得不称赞你。

B: 谢谢您这么说。

必备词汇　Necessary Vocabulary

excellent *adj.* 卓越的,极好的

appoint *v.* 指定,任命,委任

effective *adj.* 有效的

appreciate *v.* 赏识,感激

presentation *n.* 表现,表达

impressive *adj.* 给人深刻印象的

flatter *v.* 过分夸奖,奉承

put a premium 奖励

bonus *n.* 奖金,红利

Gratitude 致谢

生活中相互熟识的你我总是需要别人的帮助的，在办公室里一起工作的同事更是免不了在家长里短上给予我们帮助，得到别人的帮助后我们除了在心里默默地感激以外，还要让感激说出口。

基本句型　Sentence Patterns

I should like to express my gratitude / appreciation for . . .

我想表达我对……的感激之情。

I am very sincerely / most truly grateful to you for. . .

我真诚地为……感谢你。

I'm really grateful to you for . . .

我真的很感谢你……

Thank you for. . .

感谢你……

Many thanks for. . .

非常感谢你……

Please accept my sincere / profound appreciation for. . .

请接受我对于……的真挚/深切的感谢。

I wish to express my grateful appreciation for. . .

对……我深表感谢。

I sincerely / deeply / warmly appreciate. . .

我真挚地/深切地/亲切地感谢……

Thank you indeed from the bottom of my heart.

衷心地感谢你。

There is nothing more gratifying to me than. . .

再也没有比……更能让我感谢的了。

We were deeply touched by. . .

对……我们非常感动。

We are indebted to you. . .

我们感谢你……

I'd like to thank. . .

我要谢谢……

eHⓘw 星级典句　Classical Sentences

Thank you very much.

非常感谢。

Thank you ever so much.

太感谢你了。

I don't know how to thank you.

我真不知道如何感谢你。

Thank you anyway／all the same.

不管怎样,还是谢谢你。

Thank you most sincerely.

最真诚地感谢你。

Thanks a million.／Thanks ever so much.

万分感谢。／非常感谢。

Quite well, thank you.

谢谢你,很好。

Very well, thank you.

谢谢你,非常好。

eHⓘw 回应方式　Repartee

My pleasure.／It's my pleasure.

乐意效劳。

You are welcome.

不客气。

Think nothing of it. It was nothing.

没什么。

Delighted to be able to help.

很高兴能帮你。

Delighted to have been of assistance.

很高兴能对你有所帮助。

Not at all.

没关系。

That's all right.

没关系。

It's very kind of you to say so.

你这么说太客气了。

eHow 情景对话 Situational Dialogue

Part 1

A: Mr. John, I wish to express my grateful appreciation for helping me on the job.

B: Please don't mention it. I'm very delighted to be of help.

A: It's important for me. If not you I could not finished it on time.

B: It's very kind of you to say so.

A: But in fact you really helped me a lot.

B: I'm glad to hear that.

Part 2

A: Have you finished the work plan?

B: Yes, I have finished it. Thank you for providing me some primary datum.

A: It's very kind of you to say so. Delighted to have been of assistance. I'm just have them as luck would have it.

B: Thank you all the same.

Part 3

A: Thank you indeed from the bottom of my heart for helping me buy the ticket of Zhang Xue you's vocal concert.

B: I was glad to do so. If there's anything I can do for you, just call me.

A: Sure, I will. Thank you!

B: That's all right.

译文

Part 1

A: 约翰先生,非常感激您在工作上帮我这个忙。

B: 不用谢,我非常高兴能帮上这个忙。

A: 这对我很重要。如果不是你我不可能按时完成工作。

B: 你这么说太客气了。

A: 但是事实上你确实帮我了很多。

B: 你这么说我真高兴。

Part 2

A: 那个工作计划你做完了吗?

B: 是的,我已经完成了。谢谢你给我提供了很多主要的资料。

A: 你这么说真是太客气了。我也很高兴能帮上你。我也只是碰巧有这些材料。

B: 不管怎样,还是要谢谢你。

Part 3

A：我衷心地感谢你能帮我买到张学友演唱会的门票。

B：我很高兴,如果有事情需要我的话,就给我打电话。

A：当然,我会的。谢谢你!

B：没关系。

必备词汇　Necessary Vocabulary

gratitude　*n.*　感谢,感激

grateful　*adj.*　感激的,感谢的

profound　*adj.*　深刻的,意义深远的

gratifying　*adj.*　悦人的,令人满足的

indebted　*adj.*　负债的,感恩的

as luck would have it　碰巧

sincerely　*adv.*　真诚地

Apology 道歉

　　工作中出现失误是难免的,工作中出现摩擦也是经常的,所谓"人非圣贤,孰能无过",遇到工作中这些不顺人意之事,我们要本着有则改之,无则加勉的原则,在努力工作的前提下,我们要善于、敢于向他人道歉,无论错在何方,争执起了,就需要我们以大度去平息,道歉并不会使我们有失颜面,反而会给人留下胸襟广阔的印象。

✓eH✐w 基本句型 Sentence Patterns

Please forgive me for. . .

请原谅我……

How stupid / silly / clumsy of me for. . .

我有多蠢 / 傻 / 笨,竟然……

I'm sorry for. . .

关于……我很抱歉。

It's my fault for. . .

……是我的错。

I can't tell you how sorry I am for. . .

非常抱歉……

I'm extremely / really sorry for. . .

太抱歉了……

I'm sorry. I didn't mean for. . .

抱歉,我不是有意……的。

Please accept my apologies for. . .

对不起,就……请接受我的道歉。

I must apologize for. . .

我必须为……而道歉。

✓eH✐w 星级典句 Classical Sentences

I beg your pardon.

请原谅。

Please accept my sincere apology.

请接受我诚心诚意的道歉。

I can't tell you how sorry I am.

我真的是很抱歉。

You can not believe how sorry I am.

你不知道我感到多么抱歉。

Words cannot describe how sorry I am.

语言无法描述我对你的歉意。

I'm sorry, I didn't mean to bother you.

对不起,真不想打扰你。

I'm afraid I've brought you a lot of trouble.

恐怕我给你带来了不少麻烦。

Sorry about the inconvenience.

对不起添麻烦了。

I'm sorry for what I've done.

我为我的所作所为向你道歉。

I acted in haste, I jumped the gun.

我太急于求成,开始得太仓促了。

I overlooked some facts, I'll be more thorough.

我忽视了一些事实,我会更全面地看问题的。

I am not chary enough.

是我不够细心。

My preparation is too brash.

我的准备太仓促了。

eHow 回应方式   Repartee

To err is human。

人非圣贤,孰能无过。

That's OK.

没事儿。

Never mind.

无所谓。

Forget it.

忘掉它吧。

That's all right.

没关系。

You're forgiven.

我原谅你。

Don't worry about it.

别放在心上。

It's not your fault.

那不是你的错。

It really doesn't matter at all.

真的没关系。

OK. I accept your apology.

好吧。 我接受你的道歉。

I won't hold it against you.

我不会记仇的。

I'll give you another chance.

我再给你一次机会。

 情景对话 Situational Dialogue

Part 1

A: Hello, Jane.

B: Hello, John.

A: I come to apologize for what I said yesterday.

B: Don't think so.

A: I must make an apology for my fault.

B: It's really not necessary.

Part 2

A: Good morning, everybody. Please excuse me for being late.

B: Never mind.

A: Please accept my apologies for having delayed the work. I got in a heavy traffic jam.

B: It's not your fault. We arrive here just now as well as you.

A: I'm relieved to hear that. I will try not to be late from now on.

B: Don't worry about it.

Part 3

A: Good morning, boss.

B: Good morning.

A: Please forgive me for my bad job. I acted in haste. I jumped the gun. I am not chary enough.

B: To err is human。 Forget it and I will give you another chance.

A: Oh, thank you. I will try my best to do well the job with chariness. Apologize for my fault again.

B: That's ok!

译文

Part 1

A: 你好,珍妮。

B: 你好,约翰。

A: 我是来道歉的。请原谅我昨天所说的话。

B: 别那么认为。

A: 我必须为我的过失而道歉。

B: 真的没有这个必要。

Part 2

A: 大家早上好,请原谅我来晚了。

B: 没关系。

A: 请大家接受我为耽误工作的道歉。刚刚交通堵塞很严重。

B: 那不是你的错,我们也是刚刚到这的。

A: 听你这么一说,我就轻松多了。从今往后我会尽量准时的。

B: 别担心了。

Part 3

A: 早上好,老板。

B: 早上好。

A: 请原谅我把工作做得那么糟糕。我太急于求成,开始得太仓
   促了。我不够细心。

B: 人非圣贤,孰能无过呢。忘掉它吧,我会再给你一次机会的。

A: 哦,谢谢您。我会尽我最大的努力细心的做好工作的。再次就
   我的失误向您道歉。

B: 没事儿!

必备词汇　Necessary Vocabulary

apology *n.* 道歉

delay *v.* 耽搁

extremely *adv.* 极其地

clumsy *adj.* 笨拙的

overlook *v.* 忽视

chary *adj.* 仔细的，谨慎的

brash *adj.* 仓促的，性急的

traffic jam　交通堵塞

Congratulations 祝贺

　　朋友升职了、长工资了、喜迁新居了等等,都值得我们由衷地为之祝贺,一句祝贺也是对他人取得成就的赞赏。

✓H✓w 基本句型 Sentence Patterns

Congratulations on. . .

恭喜你!

I'd like to congratulate you on. . .

祝贺你!

May I congratulate you on. . .

允许我祝贺你……

Allow me to congratulate you on. . .

允许我向你祝贺。

Please accept my congratulations on your. . .

请接受我对你……的祝贺。

✓H✓w 星级典句 Classical Sentences

Please accept my sincere congratulations.

请接受我对你的衷心祝贺。

Well done!

干得好!

Fantastic!

妙极了!

✓H✓w 情景对话 Situational Dialogue

Part 1

A: Hi, Jane. It seems a good day to you. What's the good news?

B: I finally pass the accountant examination.

A: Oh, that's great! Please accept my sincere congratulations.

B: Thank you!

Part 2

A: Hello, Jane.

B: Hello, John.

A: I have heard that you is going to marry.

B: Oh, yes, you know the time of day. I have decided it just now.

A: Allow me to express my heartiest congratulations. And when you will have your wedding?

B: Date 1 in October. You must be coming that time.

A: Sure, I will. Thank you.

B: It is my pleasure.

Part 3

A: Congratulations! Your company is a great success!

B: Thanks.

A: You have really made a wonderful cause.

B: I'm flattered. I can't take all the credit though. I had lots of help.

译文

Part 1

A: 你好,珍妮。你今天气色不错,有什么好消息吗?

B: 我终于通过了会计师考试。

A: 那太好了,请接受我最诚挚的祝贺。

B: 谢谢!

Part 2

A: 你好,珍妮。

B: 你好,约翰。

A: 我听说你将要结婚了。

B: 哦,是的。你的消息很灵通。我是刚刚才决定的。

A: 请允许我向你表示最衷心的祝贺。你什么时候准备进行你的婚礼呢?

B: 10 月 1 日。到时候你一定要来啊。

A: 当然,我会的。谢谢你。

B: 我很荣幸。

Part 3

A: 祝贺你,你的公司取得了极大的成功。

B: 谢谢。

A: 你已经做出了令人惊奇的事业。

B: 您过奖了。这不能全部归功于我。我得到了许多人的帮助。

必备词汇　Necessary Vocabulary

congratulations *n.* 祝贺

accountant *n.* 会计师,会计员

bachelor *n.* 学士

credit *v.* 把……归功于……,信任

fantastic *adj.* 妙极了

Office Sundries 办公杂务

接电话、发传真、复印甚至打扫卫生在办公室中都是一些不起眼的小事情，但是事情虽小，如果干好的话同样可以获得领导、同事的赞赏。

eHⅡw 基本句型　　Sentence Patterns

Can I help you. . .

我能帮你……

Would you please. . .

请问你能……

Could you give me a hand to . . .

你能帮我……

It's my turn to. . .

轮到我……

eHⅡw 星级典句　　Classical Sentences

Could you give me a hand?

你能帮我一下吗？

What's the matter?

什么事儿？

What can I do for you?

你有什么需要吗？

——以上适合于普通的寻求帮助或者给予帮助

It's dirty and in disorder. Let me do it out.

这里又脏又乱，让我来打扫整理一下吧。

Is the water bottle empty? It's my turn to get it.

水瓶没有水了吗？轮到我去打水了。

——以上适合于办公室的打扫整理

Here are all the documents the manager of Finance Section required. They array by date.

这是财务部经理需要的文件,都是按日期排列的。

All documents should be sorted in order.

所有的文件都应该按顺序分类。

All the document and files are kept on the ground of different content.

所有的文件、档案都按不同内容保存。

We put one business fellows document all together but not adulterate with others.

我们把一个商业伙伴的资料全放在一起, 而不是与其他的掺和在一起。

——以上适合于办公室文件整理

I can have it copied.

我可以复印。

I was about to make a copy of this file.

我刚要复印这份文件。

Our copy machine isn't working well.

我们的复印机不太好使。

The paper jammed and it stopped working.

纸卡住了,机器也不动了。

Paper ran out.

没纸了。

Let me show you.

让我给你演示一下。

Would you like to staple these for you?

需要我帮你把这些装订上吗?

——以上适合于办公室复印工作

What's the maximum weight allowed?

最高重量限额是多少?

What is the postage for a letter to Xi'an?

邮寄到西安的信邮资是多少？

How long will it take for a letter to reach the United States?

信邮寄到美国需要多长时间？

Can I catch the last mail today?

我能赶上今天的末班邮件吗？

Do you think I should have it registered?

你看我该挂号吗？

How long does it take by regular mail?

普通邮件要多少时间？

Please send this parcel by special delivery.

请用快件寄这个包裹。

——以上适合于到邮局办理邮件业务

The e-mail you sent this morning was returned as undeliverable.

你今天上午发的电子邮件退回来了。

Are you sure the address is correct?

你确信地址是对的吗？

Would you please send this fax for me?

你能帮我发份传真吗？

Could you tell me how to operate this machine?

你能告诉我怎样使用这台机器吗？

What's the fax number?

传真号是多少？

What's the rate for a fax to America?

往美国发传真怎么付费？

——以上适合于电子邮件、传真事务

eH w 情景对话 Situational Dialogue

Part 1

A: John, would you please take me the water bottle? I am not convenient now. The office is dirty and in disorder, and I must do it out.

B: No problem. Oh, the water bottle is empty. Let me get it filled at first.

A: Thank you very much.

B: No thanks.

Part 2

A: Jane, would you like to give me a hand?

B: What is the matter?

A: How can I use the e-mail?

B: That's easy. I can show you how to use it.

A: That's great. Will it take you long time?

B: No. Let's start.

A: OK, Thank you.

Part 3

A: Hello, John, would you please copy this for me?

B: Of course. How small do you like it?

A: I want to reduce it to one twice of the original.

B: How's this one?

A: It's a little small. Can you make it any bigger?

B: Yes. What about this one?

A: It is right. Please give me four copies.

B: OK! They are finished. Here you are.

A: Thank you very much.

Part 4

A: Hello, Jane. I want to copy this, could you help me?

B: Sure. Pass on me the original file. Oh, this is too fuzzy, are you sure to copy this?

A: Because I sprinkled water carelessly on it and I only have this one, I have to copy this.

B: Oh, I try my best to help you copy clearly. How about this one?

A: It is not good. Could you scan it first, and then I can modify some content what are not clear. At last, print it?

B: Haw – haw, you are so clever. Be it so. (a moment later) It is wonderful, and it is so clear.

A: Yes. Thank you very much.

B: It's my pleasure. And I have learnt much.

Part 5

A: John, that machine company's documents have been sent here? I want to check the transactions we made with them.

B: Please wait a moment, let me see. Here you are. Do you need anything else?

A: I also need those concerning the medicine company. Have you got them?

B: Yes, they were delivered one week ago, and I received them yesterday. Here.

A: OK, thank you.

B: There are 2 letters with the document in addition.

A: Yes? What's the content about them?

B: Oh, one is greeting letter and the other is sales letters.

A: Oh, let me have a look. Beautiful envelop! Thank you, John.

B: It's my pleasure.

Part 6

A: Good morning, Jane.

B: Good morning, John. What's the matter?

A: I come to get the letters from a customer named Black. Could you check it for me?

B: Certainly! You can find the letter from the "B sort".

A: Really? How do you file and keep them?

B: I sort out the files by the first letter of the company title or the customer's name. In short, they are kept alphabetically.

A: How clever you are!

B: Thank you for you compliment. By the way, what are the files? After you have sorted them how you will deal with them?

A: Most are letters from customers and business fellows. I will send them on grounds of difference content to relevant sections, when they have handled them the letters would come back and I will file them so that we can check later.

B: Oh, I see. I have found the letter. Thank you.

A: It's my pleasure.

Part 7

A: Excuse me, Jane.

B: What's the matter?

A: There's something wrong with my e-mail. It can't be sent out successfully.

B: Let me see. Maybe you have input the wrong address.

A: No, have a look, the address is correct.

B: Er...look, you have typed a capital letter where you should have typed a small letter.

A: Oh, I see. If not you I couldn't find it till tomorrow. Thank you very much.

Part 8

A: Jane, what's brand of the electrograph in our office?

B: The new one sent yesterday? Oh, it is Epson.

A: Could you tell me how to use this machine?

B: Yes. First you should insert the paper into the machine. Then you dial the phone number of the receiving fax machine. Finally, you push this button.

A: Thank you.

B: If you want to send to another country or city, remember to dial the country code first.

A: I see. Thank you.

Part 9

A: Hi, Jane, would you please help me send this fax?

B: Sure. Where to?

A: England.

B: What is the number?

A: Here you are.

B: It seems the area code is missing.

A: Yes, because I don't know the code of England. Could you check it for me?

B: No problem. Here it is. Should I send it now?

A: Yes. Thank you.

Part 10

A: Good afternoon, Jane. Would you please get this letter out?

B: Oh, the last pick-up mail-cart is at 5: 30, it is already 5:45. I'm afraid it's too late. I think the last pick-up should have gone.

A: Really? Oh, it's too bad. Maybe next time I should be a little earlier. By the way, do you happen to have any stamps? I have no stamps on envelop.

B: Yes, I have. What par value stamps do you want?

A: One 8jiao or one 3jiao and one 5jiao.

B: Oh, sorry. I only have one 5jiao.

A: It doesn't matter. I could drop the letter into the post box on my way to our company, but then I have no stamps. Now I have to wait until the post office opens tomorrow morning.

B: Why don't you use our company's envelopes?

A: What is the difference? I still need to buy stamps.

B: No. Have a look. Postage Paid.

A: Oh, great, Jane. Thank you very much.

B: No thanks.

Part 11

A: Hello, John. I just got a letter for you from Beijing. Shall I take it to you?

B: Oh, very good, please. Maybe it is the one I have been waiting for.

A: Here you are.

B: Thank you. Are there any other things except this one for me today?

A: There hasn't been so far.

B: Would you please help me get these letters posted? This one is important and urgent. Please send it by express. The others are ordinary letters。

A: OK. Is there any information I should enclose with them?

B: Yes, there are the commercial information, financial information and sales information, when you read the answer letter you will know what the enclosures are.

译文

Part 1

A: 约翰,能帮我把水瓶拿过来吗?我现在不太方便。办公室现在又脏又乱,我必须把它收拾干净。

B: 没有问题。哦,水瓶没有水了。让我先去把水打满。

A: 多谢了。

B: 不客气。

Part 2

A: 珍妮,能帮我一下吗?

B: 什么事儿?

A: 我怎么才能使用电子邮件呢?

B: 这很简单。我给你演示一下如何使用它。

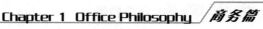

A: 那太好了,这会占用你很长时间吗?

B: 不会的。让我们开始吧。

A: 好的,谢谢。

Part 3

A: 你好,约翰,能帮我把这个复印一下吗?

B: 当然可以,你想要多大的?

A: 我想把它缩小到原件的二分之一?

B: 这张怎么样?

A: 这个有点小了。你能把它弄得稍微大一点吗?

B: 当然。这张怎么样?

A: 这张正合适。请给我复印 4 份吧。

B: 好的。复印好了。给你。

A: 非常感谢。

Part 4

A: 你好,珍妮,我想复印一下这个,你能帮我吗?

B: 当然,请把原件递给我。哦,这个有点太模糊了,你确定要复印这个吗?

A: 因为我不小心把水洒在了上面并且我就只有这么一份了,所以我不得不复印这个。

B: 哦,我尽力帮你复印清楚些。看看这张怎么样?

A: 不太好。你能先把它扫描一下,然后我可以改一下那些不清楚的内容。最后再打印出来吗?

B: 哈哈,你真是太聪明了。就这样干吧。(一会儿之后)真是太好了,而且印得这么清楚。

A: 是的。非常感谢。

B: 我很荣幸。并且我也学到了很多。

Part 5

A: 约翰,那家机器公司的文件送过来了吗？我想要核对一下我们和他们的贸易往来。

B: 请稍等,让我看一下。给你。您还要别的文件吗？

A: 对了,我还要有关那个医药公司的文件,你拿到它们了吗？

B: 是的,它们在一周以前就已经寄了,我昨天收到了它们。给你。

A: 好的,谢谢。

B: 另外随文件过来的还有两封信。

A: 是吗？这两封信的内容是什么？

B: 哦,一封是问候信,另一封是询问销售情况的信。

A: 哦,让我看一下。信封很漂亮！谢谢你,约翰。

B: 我很荣幸。

Part 6

A: 早上好,珍妮。

B: 早上好,约翰。有什么事情吗？

A: 我来这取一封来自客户 BLACK 的来信。你能帮我查一下吗？

B: 当然可以。你可以在 B 类里面找到这封信。

A: 真的吗？你是怎么样归档保管这些文件的？

B: 我把这些文件按公司名字或者是客户姓名的第一个字母来分类。简而言之,就是按字母来分类保存。

A: 你真是太聪明了！

B: 谢谢您的夸奖。顺便说一下,这些都是什么文件?在你分类以后你怎么处理这些文件呢？

A: 绝大部分是客户和商业伙伴的来信。我会根据不同的内容把它们送到相关的部门去,当他们处理完了之后就把那些文件送回到我这,我再把它们分类保存以便日后查阅。

B: 哦,我明白了。我已经找到了那封信。谢谢你。

A: 我很荣幸。

Part 7

A: 打扰一下,珍妮。

B: 什么事儿?

A: 我的电子邮件出了问题,不能成功地发送出去。

B: 让我看看。可能你的地址弄错了吧。

A: 不会的,来看看,这个地址是正确的。

B: 嗯……,看,你把应该使用小写字母的地方写成大写了。

A: 哦,我明白了,如果不是你,到明天我也发现不了。非常感谢。

Part 8

A: 珍妮,我们办公室的传真机是什么牌子?

B: 昨天送来的那台新机子吗?哦,是爱普生的。

A: 你能告诉我怎么使用这台机器吗?

首先你要把纸放进机器,然后再打对方的传真号,最后

键。

B: 如果你想往其他国家或城市发传真,那你要记住先拨国家区号。

A: 我明白了。谢谢。

Part 9

A: 你好,珍妮,请问你能帮我发个传真吗?

B: 当然可以。往哪发?

A: 英国。

B: 电话号码是多少?

A: 在这。

B: 这好像没有写区号。

A: 是的，因为我不知道英国的区号是多少。你能帮我查一下吗？

B: 没问题。我现在就给你发吗？

A: 是的。谢谢。

Part 10

A: 珍妮，中午好。请问你能帮我把这封信寄出去吗？

B: 哦，最后一班邮车是 5 点 30 分，现在已经 5 点 45 了。恐怕现在太晚了。最后一班车邮车可能已经开走了。

A: 是吗？哦，真是太糟糕了。或许下一次我应该早点。顺便问一下，你那有邮票吗？我这封信上还没有贴邮票呢。

B: 是的，我有。你想要什么面值的邮票？

A: 一张 8 角的或者是一张 3 角和一张 5 角的。

B: 哦，对不起，我只有一张 5 角的了。

A: 没有关系。我本来应该在来公司的路上把信扔进邮箱里，现在没有邮票，我只好等到明天早上邮局开门了。

B: 你为什么不用我们公司的信封呢？

A: 有什么区别吗？我还是得自己买邮票。

B: 不需要。看，邮资已付。

A: 哦，太好了，珍妮。非常感谢。

B: 不客气。

Part 11

A: 约翰先生你好。我刚刚收到从北京给你发来的一封信，要我拿来吗？

B: 噢，太好了，请拿过来吧，可能那就是我在等的那封。

A: 好的。给您。

B: 谢谢。除了这个,今天还有我的别的邮件吗?

A: 到目前为止还没有。

B: 你能帮我把这些信发出去吗? 这封是重要的急信,请用快递寄出,其他都是些普通信件。

A: 好的。还需要随信附上资料吗?

B: 是的,这有商业资料,财务资料和销售资料,等你看完我的这封回信就知道要分别附上哪些资料了。

必备词汇　Necessary Vocabulary

adulterate *v.* 掺和,掺假

jam *v.* 堵塞,塞满

run out 被用完

staple *v.* 装订

maximum *n.* 最大量,最大限度

postage *n.* 邮资

register *v.* 登记,注册,挂号

parcel *n.* 包裹

delivery *n.* 递送,交付

undeliverable *adj.* 无法投递的,无法送达的

convenient *adj.* 方便的

original *n.* 原物,原件

fuzzy *adj.* 模糊的,失真的

sprinkle *v.* 洒,喷洒

be it so 就这样吧,好吧

wonderful *adj.* 令人惊奇的,极好的

transaction *n.* 交易,事务

in short 简言之

alphabetically *adv.* 按字母顺序地

compliment *n.* 称赞,赞扬

relevant *adj.* 有关的,相应的

on grounds of 根据

handle *v.* 处理,运用

capital *adj.* 大写的

electrograph *n.* 传真机

pick-up *n.* 提取,搭便车

mail-cart *n.* 邮车

par value *n.* 票面价值,面值

postage paid 邮资已付

Chapter 2   Simple Procedures

Chapter 2 Simple Procedures

Making Appointment 预约

在商场上，时间如金钱，时间如生命，如何提高与商业伙伴的合作效率，争取到最大的发展机遇，是企业生存的关键，通过预约与商业伙伴洽谈业务已经成了一种商业习惯，把这一步铺垫好对以后进一步的合作非常有益。

基本句型 Sentence Patterns

I'm calling about. . .

我打电话是来……

May I speak to. . .

我可以和……通话吗？

I'd like to make an appointment with him to talk about. . .

我想约他和他谈谈关于……的事情。

Could I meet you sometime this week to talk about. . .

我们在这周某个时间见个面讨论……可以吗？

Could you transfer me back to. . .

请帮我转回……好吗？

Could you put me through to. . .

请帮我接……，好吗？

星级典句 Classical Sentences

Could you let me have an hour or so in the morning?

上午安排一个小时左右可以吗？

I'm looking forward to seeing you tomorrow.

盼望明天见到你。

Could you give him a message please?

你能给我传个口信吗？

Hold on a moment, please.

请不要挂线。

May I know who is calling?

请问你是哪里打来的？

Is there anything I can help?

我可以帮什么忙吗?

I really appreciate that you're interested in our products.

非常感谢你对我们的产品感兴趣。

That's very kind of you, but it's urgent. Can I talk to the vice manager?

非常感谢你。但情况紧急,请找副经理好吗?

No, thanks, I'll try his mobile phone.

不用了,谢谢。我打他手机吧。

Please have him return my call.

请叫他给我回个电话。

Tell him to give me a call when he returns.

他回来后,请他给我打个电话。

eHow 回应方式 Repartee

I'm pretty booked up these days.

我这几天时间排满了。

I'm tied up all day.

我整天都有事情。

Can I take a message?

我能带个口信吗?

Is there anything I can do for you?

有什么可以效劳的吗?

Wait a minute.

请稍等。

Hold on the line, please.

请别挂断。

Thanks for your help.

谢谢你的帮忙。

Thanks for the information.

谢谢你提供的信息。

I really appreciate your answer.

非常感谢你的答复。

I'm sorry. He has not come back yet. Do you want to leave a message to him?

很抱歉,他还没有回来。您想给他留个口信吗?

Unfortunately, he's out on business. Any message for him?

很不巧,他出差了,有口信给他吗?

eHow 情景对话 Situational Dialogue

Part 1

A: Good morning, May I speak to Jane?

B: Unfortunately, she's out on business.

A: When will she be back?

B: Sorry, I'm not sure. May I know who is calling?

A: Oh, I'm John from IBM in United States. I'd like to make an appointment with her to talk about an order of computers with your company.

B: Do you want to leave a message to her?

A: Yes. Tell her to give me a call when she returns.

B: OK. I'll tell her that as soon as he comes back.

A: Thank you very much.

B: You are welcome.

Part 2

A: China Dragon Corporation, good morning. What can I do for you?

B: Good morning. Could you put me through to John?

A: Hold on a moment, please.

B: Thank you!

C: Hello, John speaking.

B: Hello, I am Jane from San sun Corporation. Could I meet you sometime this week to talk about stocking the gym things for 2008 Beijing Olympiad.

C: Oh, I see. I really appreciate that you're interested in our products. But I'm pretty booked up these days.

B: Could you let me have an hour or so?

C: Is next Monday ok?

B: Yes, sure. What's the accurate time?

C: 9:00 next Monday.

B: I really appreciate your answer. See you next Monday.

C: See you.

译文

Part 1

A: 早上好,我可以和珍妮说话吗?

B: 很不巧,她出差了。

A: 她什么时候能回来呢?

B: 对不起,我不太清楚。我能知道是谁打来的电话吗?

A: 哦,我是美国 IBM 的约翰。我想约她谈谈关于你们公司订购电脑的事情。

B: 您想给他留个口信吗?

A: 好的。她回来后,请她给我回个电话。

B: 好的。她一回来我就转告她。

A: 非常感谢。

B: 不客气。

Part 2

A: 早上好,这里是中国龙公司。我能帮你什么吗?

B: 早上好,能帮我接一下约翰吗?

A: 别挂线,请等一下。

B: 谢谢。

C: 你好,我是约翰。

B: 你好,我是来自三森公司的珍妮。这个星期某个时候我能见见你并谈一下关于 2008 年北京奥运会采购体育用品的事情吗?

C: 哦,我明白了。非常感谢你对我们的产品感兴趣。但是我这几天的时间都已经排满了。

B: 你能给我安排大约一个小时的时间吗?

C: 下个星期一怎么样?

B: 是的,当然可以。具体是什么时间呢?

C: 下个星期一早上九点。

B: 非常感激您的答复。下个星期一见。

C: 再见。

必备词汇　Necessary Vocabulary

appointment *n.* 约会,指定

transfer *v.* 传递,转移

put through 接通

look forward to 期待,盼望

urgent *adj.* 急迫的,紧急的

vice 代理,副的

book up 预定

unfortunately *adv.* 不幸地

gym *n.* 体育,体育馆,体操

Olympiad *n.* 奥林匹克运动会

Reception 接待

　　商务接待是公司、企业形象最前卫的工作，是给客户以及合作伙伴留下的第一印象，负责接待的人员，应该抱有尊敬、友好的态度，而且在接待之前要准备好必要的文件资料，安排好行程和会谈内容，以便给远道而来的客户留下美好的印象。

eHow 基本句型 Sentence Patterns

We need to make accommodation for. . .

我们需要为……安排住宿。

They will arrive on. . .

他们将于……时候到达。

We will meet them at the airport/train station.

我们一起去机场/火车站接他们。

We need to draft an agenda for the reception.

我们要拟定一份接待日程表。

eHow 星级典句 Classical Sentences

I think we'd better check with them to find if they have any other advice or arrangements.

我想我们最好与他们沟通一下，看他们是否还有什么好的其他的建议或安排。

I'll sort the draft out.

我会把计划整理出来。

There are some trivial matters on reception, I think you should consider and try to satisfy the guests.

接待上的一些琐碎事情你要考虑到,尽量让客人满意。

Could you tell me your arrival time so that I can pick you up at the airport?

你能告诉我你的到达时间吗,我好可以去机场接你。

Would you please give me a call when you arrive?

当你到达时给我打个电话好吗?

You must be very tired after such a long flight. Shall we take you straight to the hotel?

你们长途飞行一定很累,我们直接送你们到酒店好吗?

How was you flight?

一路还好吧?

Did you have a good flight?

一路顺利吗?

I'll call you tomorrow so that we can set up a schedule of appointments, is that ok?

明天我给你打电话以便把日程安排好,可以吗?

Let me help you with your luggage.

让我来帮您提行李。

I've been looking forward to meeting you!

久仰!

Have you had a chance to arrange reservations for a room at a hotel?

您订了旅馆了吗?

I will reserve you a room.

我会帮你预定一个房间。

eHiw 情景对话　Situational Dialogue

Part 1

A: Hello, Jane.

B: Hello, John.

A: What are you busy doing?

B: Oh, I am drafting an agenda for the reception of International Corporation.

A: You mean the arrangements for their visit?

B: Yes. They will arrive on October 8. I will meet them on the airport.

A: Have the draft been done?

B: Not yet, but I'll try my best. After drafting the visiting agenda, I'll let you go through.

A: Thanks. Let them have a rest when they arrive. We can start our talks on October 10.

B: OK. Let me take down the notes.

A: Well, I think we'd better check with them to find if they have any other advice or arrangement.

B: I'll do that this afternoon.

Part 2

A: How nice to see you again, Mr. Brown.

B: Nice to meet you too. Oh, you haven't met my colleague Jane. Jane, this is Mr. John.

A: How do you do! Jane.

C: How do you do! Mr. John. I've been looking forward to meeting you!

B: Did you have a nice journey?

A: Not bad except some turbulence.

B: Well, you must be very tired after such a long flight. We have reserved you a room. Shall we take you straight to the hotel?

A: Yes, thanks. That would be best.

B: Let me help you with your luggage.

A: Oh, they are too heavy for you. I can manage.

B: OK. I'll drive our car here. Please wait a moment.

Part 3

A: Hello, Mr. John. Welcome to China. Did you have a nice trip?

B: Hello, Miss Jane. I have a wonderful trip. And this place is also exciting.

A: Have you had a chance to arrange reservations for a room at a hotel?

B: Oh, not yet.

A: It doesn't matter. We have reserved you a room, and is a five-star one opposite to our company.

B: Thank you very much. You are circumspect.

A: It's my pleasure. I'll call you tomorrow so that we can set up a schedule of appointments, is that OK?

B: OK! Could you please depict the agenda mainly in advance?

A: Certainly. You stay here for six or seven days, two day's talk, one day's visit to the Great Wall, two days' weekend, some recreation activities, one day's visit to our company. By the way, arrange some necessary meals or banquets.

B: I see. That's good. Your Chinese are precisian.

A: It's very kind of you for saying so. Now let me take you straight to the hotel.

B: Thank you very much.

A: It's my pleasure.

译文

Part 1

A: 你好,珍妮。

B: 你好,约翰。

A: 你现在在忙什么呢?

B: 我在拟定一份关于国际公司来访的接待日程表。

A: 你是指他们访问的安排吗?

B: 是的。他们将会在 10 月 8 日达到。我会去机场接他们。

A: 计划拟定好了吗?

B: 还没有,但是我会尽力的。在草拟访问的日程表以后,我会请您过目的。

A: 多谢。他们到了以后先让他们好好休息。我们 10 月 10 日开始会谈。

B: 好的。让我记一下。

A: 好的,我想最好与他们沟通一下,看他们是否还有什么其他的建议或安排。

B: 我今天下午就做这件事情。

Part 2

A: 真高兴再次见到您,布朗先生。

B: 见到你我也很高兴。哦,你还没有见过我的同事,这是珍妮。珍妮,这是约翰先生。

A: 珍妮,你好。

C: 你好,约翰先生。久仰!

B: 旅途愉快吗?

A: 还可以,除了有一些颠簸。

B: 你们长途飞行之后一定很累吧。我们已经帮您订了房间。我们直接送您到酒店好吗?

A: 好的,谢谢。这正合我意。

B: 让我帮你拿行李。

A: 哦,对您来说太重了。让我自己来吧。

B: 好吧,我把车开过来,请您稍等一下。

Part 3

A: 你好,约翰先生。欢迎来到中国。旅途还愉快吗?

B: 你好,珍妮小姐。我的旅途好极了。并且中国也是个令人兴奋的地方。

A: 您预定旅馆了吗?

B: 哦,还没有。

A: 没有关系。我们已经为您预定了一个房间,并且是个五星级的酒店,就在我们公司对面。

B: 非常感谢,你们想得很周到。

A: 我很荣幸。明天我给你打电话以便把日程安排好,可以吗?

B: 可以。你能提前告诉我一下主要的日程安排吗?

A: 当然可以。你在这呆 6~7 天,两天会谈,一天去长城,两天是周末,安排一些娱乐活动,一天参观我们公司。顺便说一下,还要安排一些必要的会餐或者宴会。

B: 我明白了,太好了。你们中国人是非常严谨的人。

A: 谢谢您能这么说。现在让我把您直接送到酒店吧。

B: 非常感谢。

A: 我很荣幸。

必备词汇　Necessary Vocabulary

accommodation *n.* 住宿，预定铺位

draft *v.* 起草，草拟

agenda *n.* 议事单，议程表

reception *n.* 接待，招待

trivial *adj.* 琐碎的

schedule *n.* 时间表，进度表

turbulence *n.* 颠簸，动荡

reserve *v.* 预定，预约

five-star *adj.* 五星的，最高级的

circumspect *adj.* 周到的，慎重的

depict *v.* 描述，叙述

in advance 预先，提前

banquet *n.* 宴会

precisian *n.* 严谨的人，严格遵守规则的人

Visit 参观

　　参观公司是商务活动中一个很重要的环节，不仅可以使客户能了解公司的运作情况、在市场中所占有的地位、增添合作的信心，在参观的同时还可以向客户介绍并展示公司的产品或者服务项目。

eHow 基本句型　Sentence Patterns

This way please.

请这边走。

Please step this way.

请走这边。

Let me take you there.

我带你去那。

I'll show you the way.

我给你指路。

We will show you. . .

我们将给您展示……

Our plant is . . . We have our . . . and so on.

我们的工厂是……,我们有自己的……,等等。

Please follow me this way. . . now here we are.

请跟我来……到了。

eHow 星级典句　Classical Sentences

Would you please put on these work clothes.

请你们穿上工作服。

If you don't mind, would you please put on the work clothes?

如果您不介意,请您穿上工作服好吗?

Please put on the safety helmet, while you enter the site.

进入工地,请戴上安全帽。

Here are some brochures. They will give you a brief account of our

company.

这里有几本小册子,这些会让你们对我们厂有个大概的认识。

Also with a lot of nice pictures.

还有很多很不错的图片。

These are new models in our country.

这些在我国市场上都是最新款的。

Is there anything else you'd like to see?

你们还想看些什么?

I'm not familiar with that part, let me call some one who is really up on that matter.

对于那部分我不太熟悉,让我请个比较了解此事的人来。

You must be tired, having seen so many places of our company. Shall we have a rest?

看了我们公司这么多地方,您一定累了吧,我们休息一下好吗?

eHow 回应方式　Repartee

This is the first time we visit your company.

这是我们第一次到你们公司参观。

They are well printed.

印刷很精美。

How big is your company?

贵公司规模有多大呢?

How is your company's market share?

贵公司的市场占有率由多少?

How many employees do you have?

贵公司有多少员工呢?

How much do they cost?

它们的价位是多少？

Can I ask some questions about. . .

我能问一些关于……的问题吗？

Your company is famed and developed very quickly in the past. . . years.

你们公司是很有名的,并且在过去……年里发展非常快。

eHｌw 情景对话 Situational Dialogue

A: Good morning, John.

B: Good morning, Jane.

A: Today we will visit our company, and I will translate for you. I hope you will have a mainly idea about our company.

B: That's OK!

A: This way please. And would you please put on these work clothes and safety helmet?

B: Certainly. You are thoughtful.

A: Here are some brochures. They will give you a brief account of our company.

B: Oh, they are well printed.

A: Thank you! Now let's go to the workshop. (a moment later) This is our workshop. You can see our company is very advanced. We even have ourselves labs, QC department, packing work-shops and so on.

B: It's wonderful. Even in Europe your equipments are very advanced, and your layout is scientific and logical.

A: As far as technology is concerned, we believe we are one-up.

B: How big is your company?

A: It's take up 5 hectare. We have 2000 employees, and about 1500 in the workshop, 150 in the office, the remains in the regions.

B: Oh, I see. How is your company's profit and trade?

A: It's the third in trading volume and the top in profit in China in this line. And we have 30% market in China.

B: Your company is famed and developed very quickly in the past 5 years. Would you mind showing us around your exhibit room?

A: Certainly. Please step this way. (a moment later) These are our company's new products which are about to coming into the market.

B: It is finely.

A: I think that's everything. Is there anything else you'd like to see?

B: No. That's enough.

A: Would you like to have a break with a cup of tea?

B: I'm glad to. Thank you.

A: It' s my pleasure.

B: Oh, may I ask any questions about the technique?

A: I'm not familiar about that part. Let me call Mr. Brown who has it at his fingers.

B: Thank you very much.

译文

A: 早上好,约翰。

B: 早上好,珍妮。

A: 今天我们要参观我们的公司,我会为您翻译。我希望在参观之后您能对我们公司有一个大体的了解。

B: 好的。

A: 这边请。请你们穿上工作服、戴上安全帽可以吗？

B: 当然可以。你们想得很周到。

A: 这里有几本小册子，这些会让你们对我们厂有个大概的认识。

B: 哦,这些小册子印刷得很精美啊。

A: 谢谢。让我们去车间吧。(一会儿之后)这就是车间了。你们能够发现我们的车间非常先进。我们甚至有自己的实验室、质检部门、包装车间等等。

B: 真是太好了。你们的设备甚至在欧洲都是非常先进的,并且你们的布局非常科学合理。

A: 就技术而言,我们是领先的。

B: 贵公司的规模有多大？

A: 整个公司占地 5 公顷。我们有 2000 员工,大约有 1500 人在车间,150 人在办公司,剩下的人在地方。

B: 哦,我明白了。你们公司的利润和贸易情况如何？

A: 在中国同行业中贸易总额第三,利润则高居第一位。在中国我们拥有 30% 的占有率。

B: 你们公司很有名并且在最近 5 年来发展很快。你介意带我到你们的产品陈列室看看吗？

A: 当然可以。请这边走。(一会儿之后)这就是我们公司即将投入市场的新产品。

B: 很精美。

A: 我想就这些了。你还想看些什么？

B: 不,已经足够了。

A: 要不要休息一下,来杯茶？

B: 非常高兴。谢谢。

A: 我很荣幸。

B: 哦,我可以问一些技术方面的问题吗？

A: 我对那部分不太熟悉。让我把布朗先生叫来,他对那部分很精通。

B: 非常感谢。

必备词汇 Necessary Vocabulary

helmet *n.* 头盔,钢盔

brochure *n.* 小册子

employee *n.* 职工,雇员

equipment *n.* 装备,设备

layout *n.* 规划,布局

logical *adj.* 合理的

one-up *n.* 领先的,占上风的

hectare *n.* 公顷

region *n.* 地方,区域

volume *n.* 量

famed *adj.* 闻名的,著名的

exhibit *n.* 展览品,陈列品

finely *adv.* 美好地,细微地

have sth. at one's fingers 精通某事物

Recreation Arrangement
安排娱乐活动

在繁忙的商务活动中,适当、适时地安排一些娱乐活动不仅可以缓解一下双方的工作压力,而且可以在娱乐中获得更多沟通的机会,增进双方的好感;这会对双方的商务会谈和业务关系起很重要的促进作用。

 基本句型　Sentence Patterns

Would you like to. . . this weekend?

周末去……好吗?

What do you feel like. . .

你们喜欢什么……

What's your favorite. . .

你们喜欢什么……

Let's go to. . . have a relaxation.

让我们去……放松一下吧。

If you have no plans for this Sunday, what about. . .

如果您这个星期天没有什么安排的话,……怎么样?

星级典句　Classical Sentences

Do you have any plan for next weekend?

这个周末有什么计划吗?

How do you relax at weekend?

你们周末怎么放松一下?

Why not have some entertainments to relax?

为什么不来些娱乐活动放松一下呢?

What do you feel like doing/playing?

你们喜欢做(玩)什么呢?

What's your favorite music/film?

你特别喜欢的音乐(电影)是什么?

What do you suggest for relaxing?

你对放松一下有什么提议吗?

Would you like to go sight-seeing this weekend?

周末出去观光一下好吗?

We have ourselves bus.

我们有自己的巴士。

I'd like to show you around in our city.

我想带您逛逛我们的城市。

If you like I would arrange a two-day-tour of Xi'an.

如果您喜欢,我会安排西安两日游。

If you have no plans this Sunday, what about visiting the Great Wall?

如果您这个星期天没有计划的话,去长城逛逛如何?

eHow 情景对话 Situational Dialogue

Part 1

A: Good afternoon, Mr. John.

B: Good afternoon, Miss. Jane.

A: We have been working hard these days. Well, if you have no plans for this weekend, why not have some entertainments to relax?

B: It's a good idea. We can recover fresh.

A: What do you suggest for relaxing?

B: We are at your disposal.

A: How about going to visit the Great Wall? And we can breathe the fresh air and take exercise.

B: That sounds great! I am looking forward to have a sight of the Great Wall at all times. It symbolizes China and it's famed all around the world. We can visit this interesting place and understand more about China.

A: OK. Let's prepare tonight and get going tomorrow.

B: All right. See you tomorrow.

A: See you tomorrow.

Part 2

A: Hello, John.

B: Hello, Jane.

A: Do you have any plan this weekend?

B: No. Not have for the moment.

A: Why not have some entertainments to relax? What sports do you feel like playing?

B: I like playing basketball, football, but my favourite is playing golf. Yes, do you have some good golf course nearby the countryside?

A: Oh, I like golf too. And I know a nice golf course near the Beijing where we can enjoy ourselves.

B: That's wonderful.

A: But we have two days rest. We can't play golf for two days. Have you others hobbies?

B: Yes, I like listening to music and seeing a film.

A: That's right. We can go to the cinema. *The World War* has been screening recently. It's a science fiction and splendid.

B: Oh, I have heard the film. But I have been busy working so that I have no time to have a look. Thank you very much for such good arrangement.

A: That's very kind of you for saying so.

译文

Part 1

A: 早上好,约翰先生。

B: 早上好,珍妮小姐。

A: 这几天大家工作都很辛苦。如果你这周末没有什么计划的话,为什么不来点娱乐活动放松一下呢?

B: 好主意。我们也可以恢复一下精力。

A: 您有什么提议吗?

B: 我们听从你们的安排。

A: 去参观长城怎么样?我们可以呼吸一下新鲜空气还能锻炼。

B: 这听起来太好了。我一直都盼望着去看一看长城。它代表了中国,并且世界闻名。我们参观这个名胜古迹,对中国的了解也会更多。

A: 好的。今天晚上我们准备一下明天出发。

B: 好的。明天见。

A: 明天见。

Part 2

A: 你好,约翰。

B: 你好,珍妮。

A: 这个周末你有什么计划吗?

B: 暂时还没有。

A: 为什么不参加点娱乐活动放松一下呢?你喜欢什么运动呢?

B: 我喜欢打篮球、踢足球,但是我最喜欢的是打高尔夫球。对了,在附近的乡村有没有好的高尔夫球场?

A: 哦,我也喜欢打高尔夫。并且我知道北京附近有一个非常好的高尔夫球场，我们可以玩得很尽兴的。

B: 那真是太好了。

A: 但是我们有两天的休息时间。我们总不能打两天的高尔夫吧。你还有什么爱好吗？

B: 是的。我喜欢听音乐和看电影。

A: 那就好。我们可以去看电影。最近正在播放《世界大战》。它是一部科幻片，拍得非常壮观。

B: 哦，我听说过这部影片。但是我一直忙于工作以至于没有时间去看。非常感谢你能有这么好的安排。

A: 您这么说真是太客气了。

必备词汇　Necessary Vocabulary

favorite *n.* 特别喜欢的人或事物

relaxation *n.* 放松

entertainment *n.* 娱乐

sight-seeing *n.* 观光,游览

disposal *n.* 安排,处理

symbolize *v.* 象征

countryside *n.* 乡下

hobby *n.* 业余爱好

cinema *n.* 电影院

fiction *n.* 小说,虚构

splendid *adj.* 壮丽的,辉煌的

Business Dinner 商务会餐

　　商务会餐是商务活动中非常重要的一个环节，很多生意都是从饭桌上谈来的。一次愉快的商务会餐也是彼此合作的好的开始，不仅仅是为了生意目的而共餐，而且也推进了双方的友谊。商务会餐包括邀请进餐、西餐、中餐等内容。

eHow 基本句型 Sentence Patterns

We'd like to hold a dinner...
我们想举办一个会餐……

May I invite you to...
我可以邀请您……

I know you like...
我知道你喜欢……

Would you like to try... or...
您是想吃……还是……

Which do you prefer... or...
……和……,你更喜欢哪个?

eHow 星级典句 Classical Sentences

I wonder if you have had any plans tonight?
不知道你们今晚有没有安排?

I wonder if you are free tomorrow evening?
不知道你们明天晚上有没有空?

I wonder if you're doing anything special tonight?
不知道你们今天晚上有没有特殊的活动?

Would you like to have dinner with me?
您愿意和我一起吃晚饭吗?

Shall we have dinner together?
我们一起进餐好吗?

I want to invite you to have a dinner.
我想邀请你们共进晚餐。

Please ask your wife to join us for dinner tonight.

请您的夫人今晚一起来。

Business is concluded on the table.

生意是在饭桌上谈成的。

What would you like to order?

您想点点儿什么？

What do you have in mind?

您想要点什么？

Which soup do you prefer?

您喜欢喝哪种汤？

Which do you prefer, tea or coffee?

来杯茶还是来杯咖啡？

What will you have for dessert?

您想吃什么点心？

What would you like to drink?

您想喝点什么？

Would you like anything else?

还要点什么吗？

The environment is really first-class.

这里的环境很高级。

I am very happy you enjoy it.

我很高兴您喜欢。

May I invite you to a dinner at a Chinese restaurant?

我想请您到中国餐馆进餐好吗？

 回应方式   Repartee

I am glad to come.

我很高兴前往。

I am delighted to come.

我很高兴前往。

We are at your disposal.

我们听从你的安排。

By what time should I be ready?

我什么时候去呢?

I'm sorry I can't come. I have already accepted another invitation.

Thanks all the same.

很抱歉,我不能来。我已另有约会。谢谢。

Thank you very much for the very enjoyable dinner.

这顿饭我吃得很愉快,真谢谢您。

Thank you for the delicious meal, and I really enjoyed it.

多谢您请我吃这么棒的菜,我真的很高兴。

情景对话   Situational Dialogue

Part 1

A: Hello, Mr. John. I'm Jane calling.

B: Hello, Miss. Jane.

A: Well, I wonder if you have had any plans tonight?

B: Not yet for the moment.

A: We'd like to hold a dinner in your honor.

B: That's very kind of you.

A: What about 6: 30 at Hilton Hotel to have a typical Chinese food? Are you convenient?

B: Yes. I am glad to come.

A: Please ask your wife to join us for dinner.

B: Thank you. I think she would be delighted to go.

A: Then I will be at the hotel at 6: 00 to pick you up.

B: Thank you very much. We look forward to seeing you tonight.

A: See you.

B: See you.

Part 2

A: Mr. John, you must be hungry after having visited the company long time. Do you?

B: Oh, yes, very hungry. And you?

A: Me too. Now let's go to the dinner. (a moment later) What would you like to drink, John?

B: I'd like a glass of beer.

A: How about Qingdao beer? It's one of the most famous beer in China.

B: Oh, I have heard it long before. Let me have a try.

A: What would you like to have?

B: I like Chinese food.

A: What's food concretely?

B: I am not familiar to the name of the food. I am at your disposal.

A: OK. Let me order dishes. Would you like anything else?

B: No. That's enough. In America our lunch is usually fast food. It won't last more than one hour.

A: But in China we have a saying "business is concluded on the table". But don't worry. Please make yourself comfortable.

B: Thank you.

Part 3

A: Hello, Mr. John. Do you have plans this evening?

B: Not yet for the moment.

A: May I invite you to a dinner at a Chinese restaurant? I know a restaurant here where delicious Chinese food is served.

B: Thank you. I am delighted to go with you. I have had Chinese food before in L. A., but till now I have been not good at using chopsticks.

A: It does not matter. I will help you.

B: Thank you very much. What kind does Chinese food include?

A: It's very abundant. There are 4 types of most famous Chinese foods in our country. They are Sichuan Food, Cantonese Food, Jiangsu Food and Shandong Food.

B: Oh, it is very interesting. If I can I want to try them all. This food is out of this world!

A: Sure. You have the chance. You can try one kind this time, and another the next time.

B: How do you eat Chinese food? How do you start?

A: Remember one sentence, "When in Rome, do as the Romans do". When we start, the host will take the chopsticks first, then the others.

B: What about drinks?

A: The host will usually take the wine firstly and all the people will stand up, then the host will have a toast, then they will say "cheers" all together. The host usually bottoms up and the guests will follow. But if you can't drink, you can sip a little.

B: It's very interesting. I have learnt a lot about Chinese food from you today. Thank you very much.

A: It's very kind of you for saying so.

译文

Part 1

A: 你好,约翰先生。我是珍妮。

B: 你好,珍妮小姐。

A: 您今天晚上有什么安排吗?

B: 暂时还没有。

A: 我们想为您设宴洗尘。

B: 谢谢。

A: 6点半在希尔顿饭店吃典型的中国菜怎么样?那个时间您方便吗?

B: 是的。我很高兴前往。

A: 请您的夫人一同前往。

B: 谢谢。我想她会很高兴和我一起去的。

A: 那么我就六点到酒店来接你。

B: 非常感谢。期望着今晚能见到你们。

A: 到时见。

B: 再见。

Part 2

A: 约翰先生,参观公司这么长时间您一定饿了,是吗?

B: 哦,是的。非常饿。你呢?

A: 我也是。我们一起去吃饭吧。(一会儿之后)约翰,你想喝点什么？

B: 我想喝杯啤酒。

A: 青岛啤酒怎么样？它是中国最著名的啤酒之一了。

B: 哦，我很久以前就听说过了。让我试一试。

A: 您想吃点什么呢？

B: 我喜欢吃中国菜。

A: 具体什么菜呢？

B: 我对菜的名字不是很熟悉。我听从你的安排。

A: 好吧，让我来点菜吧。你还要其他什么吗？

B: 不，已经足够了。在美国我们的午餐一般吃快餐。通常不会超过一个小时。

A: 但是在中国我们有一个说法就是"生意是在饭桌上谈出来的"。但是别担心，请不要拘束。

B: 谢谢。

Part 3

A: 你好，约翰先生。您今天晚上又安排吗？

B: 暂时还没有呢。

A: 我可以请您一起去吃中国菜吗？我知道这有一家中国餐馆，菜的味道很不错。

B: 谢谢。我很高兴前往。我以前在洛杉矶时吃过中国菜，但是到现在为止我仍然用不好筷子。

A: 没有关系。我会帮你的。

B: 非常感谢。中国菜都包括什么种类呢？

A: 非常丰富。在我们国家有四大名菜系，川菜、粤菜、苏菜和鲁菜。

B: 哦，真是很有意思。如果可能的话我想都尝试一下。这些食物只有天上才有。

伶牙俐齿 英语口语

A: 当然可以。你有机会的。你这次可以尝试一种,等下次再尝试另一种。

B: 你们是怎么吃中国菜的,你们是怎么开始的?

A: 记住一句话就可以了,"入乡随俗"。当我们开席之后,主人先动筷子,然后其他人再动。

B: 喝酒呢?

A: 主人会先端起酒杯然后其他人都会站起来,然后主人会先说一些祝福的话,然后大家一起说"干杯"。主人通常会一饮而尽,客人也是一样的。但是如果你不能喝,你可以少喝一点。

B: 非常有趣。今天从你这学到了很多关于中国菜的知识。非常感谢。

A: 您这么说真是太客气了。

必备词汇　Necessary Vocabulary

conclude v. 决定,做出结论

soup n. 汤

dessert n. 甜品,点心

restaurant n. 餐馆,饭店

enjoyable adj. 令人愉快的,可享受的

delicious adj. 美味的

concretely adv. 具体地

chopstick n. 筷子

abundant adj. 丰富的,充裕的

sip v. 吮吸

Seeing Off 送行

天下没有不散的宴席，商务活动也同样如此。在经过繁忙的商务活动之后，抱着尊敬、友好、礼貌的态度为商业伙伴送行，美好的回忆、友善的话语都会给对方留下深刻的印象，也为今后的商业合作做好铺垫。

eHow 基本句型 Sentence Patterns

See you.

再见。

Goodbye.

再见。

So long.

再见。

——以上适合于经常见面的人之间的告别

Take care of yourself.

保重。

Good-bye then, and all the very best.

那么就再见了,万事如意。

Remember to drop me a line.

别忘了给我写信。

All the best.

万事如意。

Have a good day.

祝你过得愉快。

Remember me to your family.

代问你全家好。

I hope you have a pleasant journey home.

祝您归途一路顺风 。

Goodbye, have a nice flight.

再见,祝飞行愉快。

Have a safe trip back.

祝平安返家。

I hope to see you again.

希望能再见到您。

I will be in touch.

保持联络。

Good night then.

那么就祝你晚安吧。

Remember to look me up if ever you're here.

如果你再来这里，别忘了来看我。

——以上适合于朋友和商务伙伴

eHw 星级典句　Classical Sentences

Thank you for everything, we had a wonderful time here.

谢谢所有的招待，我们在这过得很愉快。

Come and see me when you have time.

有空时请过来。

Let's get together again in the near future.

让我们不久再聚吧。

I'm looking forward to seeing you again.

希望不久后再次见到您。

It's very nice of you to come and see me off.

您来给我送行，真是太客气了。

Have a pleasant journey and good luck.

祝旅途愉快、平安。

eHow 情景对话 Situational Dialogue

A: Times goes quickly and all good things must come to an end. It's time for me to go back to America.

B: Yup. I hope you have lived through a good time here.

A: Certainly. Thanks for everything, we have had a wonderful time in Beijing.

B: I am delighted to hear that. I'm looking forward to seeing you again.

A: Welcome to America for business. There I will invite you to taste delicious America food.

B: Thank you very much for saying so. If there is a chance, I will consider that.

A: I must go. Let's get together again in the near future. And it's very nice of you to come and see me off.

B: Have a pleasant journey and good luck. Please keep in touch.

A: Sure. I will. Goodbye!

▶ 译文

A: 时间过得真快,天下没有不散的宴席。到了我回美国的时候了。

B: 是啊。我希望你在这度过了一段美好的时光。

A: 当然是的。谢谢你们所有的招待,我在北京过得很愉快。

B: 听您这么说我很高兴,期望能再次见到您。

A: 欢迎你们来美国洽谈业务。在那我会邀请你们品尝美味的美国菜。

B: 谢谢您这么说。如果有机会我会考虑的。

A: 我得走了。让我们在不远的将来再见吧。并且感谢你们来为我送行。

B: 祝您旅途愉快、平安。请保持联系。

A: 当然,我会的。再见!

必备词汇　Necessary Vocabulary

drop a line 写信给某人

have a pleasant journey 一路顺风,一路平安

flight *n.* 飞机的航班

look up 拜访,尊敬

see off 送行

yup *int.* 是,是的

journey *n.* 旅行,旅程

Chapter 3   Outgoing Affairs

Chapter 3   Outgoing Affairs

Booking Ticket 订机票／火车票

　　商务活动讲求守信、守时，任何一方都有着自己的工作安排，合作伙伴双方约定洽谈业务的时间一旦约定后就很难改变，预定机票、火车票对于做好出行准备、及时出行就显得非常重要了。

eHow 基本句型　Sentence Patterns

I want to fly to. . .

我想要飞到……

I want to go. . . and I'd prefer a morning flight.

我想要去……我想要一个早上的航班。

Check-in time is. . .

检票时间是……

You have to be there. . .

你要……到那。

I'd like to make a reservation to. . .

我想预订一张到……的票。

What flights do you have from. . . to. . .

从……到……都有什么航班？

Do you fly to. . . on Sunday?

星期天到……有航班吗？

eHow 星级典句　Classical Sentences

What time do I have to be at the airport?

我应该什么时候到机场呢？

I'll need an economy ticket with an open return.

我想要一张经济舱，并且是往返票的。

What time should I check in?

我应该什么时间检票呢？

I'd like to travel first-class.

我想要头等舱。

When should I get to the airport?

我应该什么时候到机场呢？

I don't want a night flight.

我不想要夜间航班。

When am I supposed to check in?

我应该什么时候检票呢？

eHow 回应方式　Repartee

Let me see what's available.

让我看看有什么票。

Just a second and I'll check the schedule.

请稍等，我看一下时间表。

One moment, please, and I'll find out what's available.

请等一下，让我查一下还有什么航班。

Just a minute and I'll see if there are any flights.

请稍等，我看是否有航班。

We have a nonstop flight leaving. . .

从……我们有一班直达航班。

eHow 回应方式　Repartee

Part 1

A: Do you fly to Tibet on Sunday?

B: Just a minute and I'll see if there are any flights.

A: By the way, I don't want a night flight.

B: There's a DC – 10 out of Baiyun Airport at 9: 15.

A: When am I supposed to check in?

B: Try to be there by 8: 15 the airport will be crowded.

Part 2

A: I'd like to make a reservation to Beijing for next Monday.

B: Just a second and I'll check the schedule.

A: I'll need an economy ticket with an open return.

B: There is a fight leaving at 9: 25.

A: I guess that's OK. What time should I check in?

B: You have to be there half an hour before departure time.

Part 3

A: I want to fly to Xi'an on Thursday.

B: Let me see what's available.

A: I'd prefer a morning flight.

B: South Flight 102 leaves at 9: 20.

A: That's fine. What time do I have to be at the airport?

B: Check-in time is 8: 45.

Part 4

A: What flights do you have from Beijing to Shanghai tomorrow?

B: One moment, please, and I'll find out what's available.

A: I'd like to travel first-class.

B: OK. We have a nonstop flight leaving Beijing at 9: 25.

A: When should I get to the airport?

B: Please be there by 8: 45 at the latest.

译文

Part 1

A: 星期天有没有飞往西藏的航班?

B: 请等一下,让我看看是否有航班。

A: 顺便说一声,我不想要夜间的航班。

B: 在白云机场有一航班 DC – 10 早上 9:15 起飞。

A: 我应该什么时候检票呢?

B: 尽量 8:15 到那吧,飞机场人会很多的。

Part 2

A: 我想预订一张下星期一到北京的票。

B: 请稍等一下,让我查一下。

A: 我想要一张往返的经济舱机票。

B: 有一班在早上 9:25 离开。

A: 我想就那个了。我应该什么时候检票呢?

B: 你应该在飞机起飞之前半个小时到那。

Part 3

A: 我想要在星期四飞往西安。

B: 让我看看有什么航班。

A: 我想要早班航班。

B: 南方航班 102 在 9:20 起飞。

A: 那太好了。我应该什么时候到机场呢?

B: 8:45 检票。

Part 4

A: 明天从北京到上海都有什么航班?

B: 请稍等,我查一下都有什么航班。

A: 我想要头等舱。

B: 好的。我们有一班 9:25 从北京直达上海。

A: 我应该什么时候到机场呢?

B: 请最晚在 8:45 以前到。

必备词汇　Necessary Vocabulary

check-in *n.* 报到处,登记处

reservation *n.* 保留,预定,预约

first-class *n.* 头等舱

Tibet *n.* 西藏

crowded *adj.* 拥挤的,塞满的

departure *n.* 启程,出发,离开

available *adj.* 可用到的,可利用的

nonstop *adj.* 不断的

Booking Room 订旅馆

　　出差来到某地往往人生地不熟,再要自己跑着找旅馆,万一在节庆人多的时候, 跑了多家旅馆也可能找不到合适的房间, 所以在出差之前把旅馆订好便可以高枕无忧, 一心准备业务活动。

eHow 基本句型 Sentence Patterns

I want to reserve a room with . . . .

我想预订一间有……的房间。

I'd like to make a reservation of room with . . .

我想预订一个……的房间。

I'd like to book a single room with……

我想订一间有……的单人间。

What's the price difference?

两种房间的价格有什么不同?

We will be leaving . . .

我们会……(什么时候)退房。

What's the price, please?/What's the rate, please?

请问房费是多少?

That sounds not bad at all. I'll take it.

听起来还不错,这个房间我要了。

Do you have anything bigger (better/cheaper)?

是否还有更大(更好/更便宜)的房间?

I'll take this room.

我就订这个房间。

Do you accept credit cards?

这里可以使用信用卡吗?

May I see the room?

我可以看看房间吗?

Could you keep my valuables?

是否可代为保管贵重物品?

What time does the dining room open?

餐厅几点开始营业?

Is there a beauty salon?

旅馆内有美容院吗?

When is check-out time?

何时需退房?

H·w 星级典句 Classical Sentences

By the way, I'd like a quiet room away from the street if it is possible.

顺便说一下,如有可能我想要一个不临街的安静房间。

I think I'll take the one with a front view.

我想我还是要阳面的吧。

I'd like a quiet room.

我想要安静一点的房间。

I'd like a room on the upper level.

我想要楼上的房间。

I'd like a room with a nice view。

我想要一个视野好点的房间。

H·w 情景对话 Situational Dialogue

Part 1

A: Great Wall Hotel, what can I do for you?

B: I'd like to book a double room next Sunday.

A: Wait a minutes, I will check if there is available.

B: Thank you.

A: Yes. There are two kinds of double rooms including general rooms and standard rooms. What kind do you need?

B: What's the price difference?

A: A double room with a front view is 300yuan per night, one with a rear view is 250yuan per night.

B: I think I'll take the one with a front view then.

A: How long will you be staying?

B: It's not determined.

A: And we look forward to seeing you next Sunday.

B: Thank you.

Part 2

A: I'd like to book a single room with bath from October 1 to 7.

B: We do have a single room available for those dates.

A: What is the rate, please?

B: The current rate is 150yuan per night. But when the National Day is coming the price will arise to 200yuan per night.

A: Is hot water available any time?

B: Yes. We provide hot water for 24 hours.

A: Do you accept credit cards? Could you keep my valuables?

B: Yes. We have special persons who are with responsibility for taking charge.

A: That sounds not bad at all. I'll take it. By the way, I'd like a quiet room away from the street if it is possible. I'd like a room with a nice view.

B: What's your name?

A: My name is John. I'll arrive late, but please keep my reservation.

B: No problem. And we look forward to seeing you.

A: Thank you!

译文

Part 1

A: 这里是长城旅馆,我能帮您什么忙?

B: 我想要在下个星期天订一个双人间。

A: 请稍等一下,我看看有没有合适的房间。

B: 谢谢。

A: 有的。这有两种类型的双人间,一种是普通间,一种是标准间。您需要哪种呢?

B: 两种类型的价格有什么不同呢?

A: 一间双人房朝阳面的每晚 300 元,朝阴面的每晚 250 元。

B: 我想我还是要阳面的吧。

A: 你们将要在这住几天?

B: 还没有决定。

A: 我们盼望下周日见到您。

B: 谢谢。

Part 2

A: 我想订一个能够洗澡的单间,从 10 月 1 日到 7 日。

B: 我们确实有一个单间,在这段时间可以用。

A: 请问房费多少?

B: 目前的费用是 150 元一个晚上,但是你知道国庆马上就要到了,所以价格会涨到 200 元一个晚上。

A: 那里随时都供应热水吗?

B: 是的,我们 24 小时提供热水。

A: 可以用信用卡吗? 可以保管我的贵重物品吗?

B: 当然可以,我们有专门的人来看管这些东西。

A: 那听起来不错,我想订一个不临街但视野好一点的安静房间。

B: 请留下您的姓名。

A: 我的名字叫约翰,我会来晚一些,请别忘了给我留房间。

B: 没问题,随时恭候您的光临。

A: 谢谢!

必备词汇 Necessary Vocabulary

rate *n.* 价格,费用

salon *n.* 沙龙

check-out *n.* 付账离开,结账

standard *adj.* 标准的,权威的,第一流的

general *adj.* 一般的,普通的

double room *n.* 双人房

rear *adj.* 后面的,背面的

take charge 看管,负责

At the Airport 在机场
In the Train Station 在火车站

 基本句型　Sentence Patterns

I have nothing to declare.

我没有要申报的东西。

Do you have anything to declare?

你有东西要申报关税吗?

May I have a customs declaration form, please?

请给一份通关申报表好吗?

Is this within the tax-free limit?

这个在免税限额内吗?

It's all personal effects.

这些东西都是我私人用的。

Can I bring this on the plane?

这件我可以带上飞机吗?

We waited for John in the lobby of the airport.

我们在机场的大厅里等约翰。

I hope you have a good trip.

祝你旅途愉快。

May I have baggage tags?

请给我行李标签好吗?

I checked my baggage in the baggage section.

我在行李房托运行李。

I won't check this baggage.

这件行李我不托运。

I'm looking for my baggage.

我正在找我的行李。

Where can I get my baggage?

我到哪里去拿我的行李呢？

Could you help me find my baggage?

请你帮我找我的行李好吗？

He guessed the train would come in early.

他猜想火车会很早到达。

The stations are always full of people.

火车站里经常挤满了人。

Where am I supposed to pay the excess train fare?

我应该在哪里补票？

Where is the ticket office?

售票处在哪儿？

How long is the ticket valid?

这车票有效期多久？

Where is immigration?

入境处在什么地方？

What's the purpose of your visit?

你旅行的目的是什么？

Could you please give me the departure time?

你能告诉我出发的时间吗？

Is the departure time on schedule?

起飞时间准时吗？

How long will the flight be delayed?

班机延误多长时间？

What's the cause of the delay?

什么原因延误？

Will the flight be delayed?

这班机会延误吗？

Excuse me, what time will the plane arrive in Tokyo?

对不起,请问飞机何时到达东京呢?

What time should I be at the departure gate?

我应该在什么时间到登机口?

May I have a disembarkation card?

请给我一张离机卡好吗?

Will the flight be canceled?

这班机会被取消吗?

From which station does the train leave?

这列火车从哪个站开出呢?

What time does the first train to Boston leave?

第一班去波士顿的列车什么时间开出呢?

Is it direct train?

这是直达车吗?

eHw 情景对话 Situational Dialogue

Part 1

A: Hello, sir. Do you have anything to declare?

B: I have nothing to declare. It's all personal effects.

A: But you have 10 mobile phones in your baggage.

B: Is this not within the tax-free limit?

A: Certainly.

B: Oh. Sorry. May I have a customs declaration form, please?

A: Here you are.

B: Thank you very much.

Part 2

A: Hello, Jane, I'm Brown speaking. What are you doing?

B: We waited for John in the lobby of the airport.

A: Where is he?

B: He is looking for his baggage.

A: Oh, I am coming to find him.

(a moment later)

A: Hi, John, have you found your baggage?

B: Not yet, Brown. Where can I get my baggage? And could you help me find my baggage?

A: Don't worry. It could not be lost. We can call the policemen at the airport, and I think they could tell us where your baggage is discharge.

B: It's a good idea. Let's go. If not you I could have had no idea.

A: Don't think so.

Part 3

A: Hello, my ticket is lost. Where am I supposed to pay the excess train fare?

B: You can go to the ticket office.

A: Where is the ticket office?

B: Over there.

A: Thank you. By the way, where is immigration?

B: Besides the ticket office. You can find a indicator.

A: Thank you again.

Part 4

A: Hello, could you please give me the departure time of DC − 107?

B: Yes, it will take off at 10 o'clock.

A: Will the flight be delayed? Is the departure time on schedule?

B: It will take off on time according to the schedule.

(a moment later)

The broadcasting at the airport: I am sorry to tell that the DC – 107 will be delayed.

A: How long will the flight be delayed?

B: Sorry, I don't know. It is not decided by me.

A: What's the cause of the delay?

B: I think it is the heavy fog.

A: How long is the ticket valid? Can it be overdue?

B: Take it easy. It has 3 days' period of validity.

A: Will the flight be canceled?

B: I don't think so.

A: What time should I be at the departure gate?

B: Calm down, please. The broadcasting will inform you before it takes off.

A: Thank you.

Part 5

A: Have you arrived at the train station?

B: Yes. The stations are full of people. I guess the train would come in early.

A: Have you checked your baggage in the baggage section?

B: I won't check this baggage. I can bring it with me.

A: What time does the first train to Beijing leave?

B: 8:00 in the afternoon.

A: Is it direct train?

B: Yes. The train is Z20 which is nonstop.

A: That's wonderful.

译文

Part 1

A: 你好,先生。您有什么东西需要报税吗?

B: 我没有需要报税的东西。这些都是私人用品。

A: 但是在你的行李里面有 10 个移动电话。

B: 难道这个不在免税范围之内吗?

A: 当然不在了。

B: 哦,对不起。请给一份通关申报表好吗?

A: 给你。

B: 非常感谢。

Part 2

A: 你好,珍妮。我是布朗。你现在在干什么?

B: 我在机场大厅里等约翰。

A: 他去哪了?

B: 他去找他的行李去了。

A: 哦,我现在就去找他。

（一会儿之后）

A: 你好,约翰,你找到你的行李了吗?

B: 还没有呢,布朗。我在哪能找到我的行李呢?你能帮我找找我的行李吗?

A: 不要担心,你的行李不会丢的。我们能给机场警察打电话,我想他们应该能够告诉我们你的行李被卸在哪了。

B: 好主意。走。如果不是你我真的没有主意了。

A: 不要这么说。

Part 3

A: 你好,我的票丢了。我应该去哪补票呢?

B: 你可以去补票处补票。

A: 补票处在哪?

B: 就在那边。

A: 谢谢。顺便问一下,入境处在哪?

B: 就在售票处的旁边。你能发现有个指示器。

A: 再次表示感谢。

Part 4

A: 你好,你能告诉我 DC – 107 离开的时间吗?

B: 当然,它会在 10 点起飞。

A: 这班机会延误吗? 起飞时间准时吗?

B: 根据时间表来看它会准时起飞。

(一会儿之后)

机场广播:非常抱歉地通知您,DC – 107 航班将要推迟起飞。

A: 班机延误多长时间?

B: 对不起,我不清楚。这个不是由我决定的。

A: 推迟的原因是什么?

B: 我想是因为大雾吧。

A: 票的有效期是多长时间? 不会过期吧?

B: 别担心。它有 3 天的有效期呢。

A: 这趟航班会被取消吗?

B: 我认为不会。

A: 我应该什么时间到登机口?

B: 请放松点。在飞机起飞以前机场广播会通知大家的。

A: 谢谢。

Part 5

A: 你到火车站了吗？

B: 是的。火车站了里人很多。我猜火车会很早到达。

A: 你在行李房托运行李了吗？

B: 这件行李我不托运了。我可以随身带着它。

A: 第一列去北京的火车什么时候开？

B: 下午 8：00.

A: 是直达车吗？

B: 是的。这趟车是 Z20,中间是不停站的。

A: 那真是太好了。

必备词汇　Necessary Vocabulary

declare *v.*（向海关）申报进口应纳税之货物

customs declaration form 通关申报表

tax-free *adj.* 免税的,无税的

personal *adj.* 私人的,个人的,针对个人的

lobby *n.* 大厅,休息室

tag *n.* 标签,标记符

valid *adj.* 有效的,有根据的

immigration *n.* 移居入境,外来的移民

discharge *v.* 卸下,放出

indicator *n.* 指示器

take off 起飞

fog *n.* 雾,烟雾,尘雾

overdue *adj.* 过期的,迟到的

period of validity 有效期

validity *n.* 有效性,合法性,正确性

Business Trip 出差

在外出差大情小事必然不少,无论是乘飞机、坐火车还是到了旅馆等,做好充足的准备以应对任何情况以及能够及时、充分地与人交流,不仅可以使一些问题迎刃而解,也可以缓解旅行的孤独感觉。

eHｗ 基本句型 Sentence Patterns

Can I stop over on the way?

我在中途可以停吗?

Does this bus go to the train station?

这辆汽车去火车站吗?

How long is the ride?

路程有多远呢?

Is this the bus for . . .

这辆公共汽车到……吗?

How long does it take to get there?

到那要多长时间呢?

Is this the right bus for. . .

这辆车是去……

——以上适合于乘坐公共汽车

Baiyun Airport, please. I have to be there by 7: 00.

白云机场,谢谢。我得在 7 点之前到那。

Do you think you can get me to Union station by 8: 00?

在 8 点之前你能把我送到联合车站吗?

Grand Central Station, please. I want to try to catch a 6: 00 train.

盛大中心车站。我得赶 6 点的火车。

——以上适合于乘坐出租汽车

The train is comfortable.

坐火车很舒服。

I can't miss the ten o'clock train. I'm going to Beijing on business.

我不能错过 10 点的火车,我要因公去北京。

——以上适合于坐火车

eHow 星级典句 Classical Sentences

I'm sure it's with the boss again this time.

我确定这次又是和老板一起。

Nothing is more stressful than going on a business trip with our boss.

没有什么比和老板一起进行商务旅行更令人有压力的。

There're still several things that haven't been decided yet before the trip.

在出发之前仍然有几件事情还没有决定。

Don't you think it a good thing for you to get out of the office for a couple of days?

你认为离开办公室一些天对你来说是一件好事情吗？

The train isn't crowded at all recently.

火车近来人不多。

Last time I went on a business trip with the boss, I didn't even have enough to eat.

上次我和老板一起商务旅行，我甚至都没有吃饱。

You don't know how tight the schedule is for this business trip.

你不知道这次商务旅行的时间有多紧。

Quite often we have to play host to them though it's their home ground.

有多少次我们不得不扮演主人的角色，尽管是在他们的地盘上。

Nothing's been decided yet. Why going there in such a hurry?

什么事情也没有决定呢。为什么要这么急着去那呢？

The company is sometimes very cheap on the travel expenses.

在旅行花费上这个公司经常很吝啬的。

I like to take an occasional business trip for a change.

我喜欢偶尔出差以有所改变。

On this trip I have to visit several important customers.

在这次旅行中我不得不拜访几个重要的客人。

We always discuss business matters. It's boring.

我们经常讨论商业事务。很令人烦恼的。

Every time I'm back, I have to write a detailed report of the business trip.

每次我回来,我都不得不写一份关于商务旅行的详细报告。

Business trip is tiring to me.

商务旅行使我很疲劳。

She always gets some presents from other people in the office when she's back from a business trip.

当她商务旅行回来后她经常会收到办公室其他人送给她的一些礼物。

——以上适合于讨论出差适宜

We'd better stop and rest pretty soon.

我们最好停下来好好休息一下。

The first thing you'll do is look for a comfortable hotel.

你要做的第一件事情就是找一家舒适的旅馆。

Do you think we'll have any trouble finding a room for the night?

你认为我们今晚找房间会不会遇到什么麻烦?

How about staying at a hotel in a city tonight?

今晚我们住城里的旅馆怎么样?

I think we should try to find a reasonable motel tonight.

我想今晚我们应该找一家合适的汽车旅馆。

I hope we can find a cheap place to spend the night.

我希望我们能找到一个便宜的住处来度过今晚。

Do you have any vacancies?

你这有空房间吗？

Do you have a single room for two nights?

你这有能住两个晚上的单人房间吗？

Do you have a double room with twin beds?

你这有有两床被子的双人房间吗？

Will you bring the laundry in if it rains?

下雨时请你收一下衣服,好吗？

Won't you iron this shirt for me?

可以帮我熨这件衬衫吗？

Could you take me a washcloth?

能帮我拿条毛巾来吗？

——以上适合于在旅馆

 情景对话   Situational Dialogue

Part 1

A: Does this bus go to the train station?

B: Yes. The terminus is the train station.

A: How long is the ride?

B: It is about 15 kilometers.

A: I can't miss the ten o'clock train. I'm going to Beijing on business. How long does it take to get there?

B: It will take 30 minutes to get there.

A: I think I must take a taxi.

   (a moment later)

A: Taxi!

C: Where are you going to?

A: Xi'an train station, please. I have to be there by 10: 00.

C: I can't promise anything, but I'll do my best.

（a moment later）

C: We have arrived. You've got plenty of time. That's 20yuan, please.

A: Thank you very much.

Part 2

A: Hello, John.

B: Hello, Jane.

A: I have heard of that you will be about to Beijing on business.

B: Yes. I like to take an occasional business trip for a change.

A: Don't you think it a good thing for you to get out of the office for a couple of days?

B: Sure. Occasional business travel could make one fresh.

A: That's sounds rational. But do you know you will be with our boss this time?

B: What? My god! Nothing is more stressful than going on a business trip with our boss. Last time I went on a business trip with the boss I didn't even have enough to eat.

A: Haw – haw. You should take it easy, so you can have a comfortable and joyful trip.

B: I will try to be. There're still several things that haven't been decided yet before the trip.

A: Why going there in such a hurry? You should handle them as soon as possible. When you arrive in Beijing, you can have some free time to have sightseeing.

B: You don't know how tight the schedule is for this business trip. On this trip I have to visit several important customers.

A: So you will have a strenuous trip. Have a nice trip.

B: Thank you very much.

Part 3

(on a train)

A: How do you do. My name is Jane.

B: How do you do. I am Brown.

A: The train isn't crowded at all recently.

B: Yes. The train is comfortable.

A: Where are you going to?

B: I am going to Beijing to have a tour.

A: That's wonderful.

B: How about you?

A: I also go to Beijing, but I am on business.

B: On business? It must be interesting.

A: Interesting? Oh, no. When I arrive in Beijing, I will meet the customers. We always discuss business matters. It's boring.

B: I think your customers will entertain you with open arms and thoughtful.

A: I hope they will. But quite often we have to play host to them though it's their home ground.

B: Really? It's too bad. But when you go back to your company you can have a relaxation.

A: No. Every time I'm back, I have to write a detailed report of the business trip. Business trip is tiring to me.

B: Does your company give you a bonus of the business trip?

A: Our company is sometimes very cheap on the travel expenses.

B: Is there anything cheering about the business trip?

A: Certainly have. I always get some presents from other people in the office when I'm back from a business trip.

B: That's good.

Part 4

A: We'd better stop and rest pretty soon.

B: Yes. I hope we can find a cheap place to spend the night.

A: Do you think we'll have any trouble finding a room for the night?

B: I don't think so. In this city there are lots of hotels. Look, there is one.

A: Let's go to have a look.

(a moment later)

A: Do you have any vacancies?

C: Yes. What kind do you need?

A: I need a standard room with bath room.

C: We have the room available. 200yuan per night.

A: Have you any cheaper to show us?

C: Yes. This way please.

(a moment later)

A: Hi, waiter.

D: What can I do for you, sir?

A: Could you take me a washcloth? By the way, won't you iron this shirt for me?

D: No problem.

A: Thank you very much. I will fetch the shirt at the counter.

D: OK.

译文

Part 1

A: 这辆公共汽车到火车站吗?

B: 是的。终点站就是火车站。

A: 路程有多远?

B: 大约有 15 公里。

A: 我不能错过 10 点的火车。我还要去北京出差。到那要多长时间。

B: 到那要用 30 分钟。

A: 我想我必须得坐出租车去了。

（一会儿之后）

A: 出租车!

C: 您想要去哪啊?

A: 请送我到西安火车站。我得在 10 点之前到那。

C: 我不能跟你承诺任何事情,但是我会尽力的。

（一会儿之后）

C: 我们到了。你还有足够的时间。一共是 20 元。谢谢。

A: 非常感谢。

Part 2

A: 你好,约翰。

B: 你好,珍妮。

A: 我听说你要去北京出差了。

B: 是的,我喜欢偶尔出差以有所改变。

A: 你认为离开办公室一些天对你来说是一件好事情吗?

B: 当然。偶尔的商务旅行能使人精神倍增。

A: 听起来很有道理。但是你知道这次你会和老板一起去吗？

B: 什么？我的上帝啊！没有什么比和老板一起进行商务旅行更令人有压力的。上次我和老板一起商务旅行，我甚至都没有吃饱。

A: 哈哈。你应该放松一点，这样你才会有个舒适和愉悦的旅行的。

B: 我会尝试着去放松的。在出发之前还有几件事情还没有决定。

A: 为什么去得这么急呢？你应该尽快把他们处理完。到北京以后你可以有一些闲暇的时间去观光一下。

B: 你不知道这次商务旅行的时间有多紧。在这次旅行中我不得不拜访几个重要的客人。

A: 那你这次旅行一定很紧张了。祝你一路顺风。

B: 非常感谢。

Part 3

（在火车上）

A: 你好，我叫珍妮。

B: 你好，我叫布朗。

A: 近来火车上人不多。

B: 是的。坐火车很舒服。

A: 你要去哪？

B: 我要去北京旅游。

A: 真是太棒了。

B: 你呢？

A: 我也去北京，但是我是去出差。

B: 出差，一定很有趣吧。

A: 有趣？哦，不是的。到了北京我就要去见我的客户。我们经常讨论商业事务。很令人烦恼的。

B: 我想你的客户会热情而周到地款待你的。

A: 我希望他们会。有多少次我们不得不扮演主人的角色,尽管是在他们的地盘上。

B: 真的吗? 那真是太糟糕了。但是当你回到你们公司后你就可以放松一下了。

A: 不会的。每次我回来,我都不得不写一份关于商务旅行的详细报告。出差对我来说是一件烦恼的事。

B: 你们公司会给你出差补贴吗?

A: 在旅行花费上我们公司经常很吝啬的。

B: 难道在商务旅行方面就没有令人高兴的事情吗?

A: 当然有了。当我商务旅行回来后我经常会收到办公室其他人送给我的一些礼物。

B: 那真好。

Part 4

A: 我们最好停下来好好休息一下。

B: 好的。我希望我们能找到一个便宜的住处来度过今晚。

A: 你认为我们今晚找房间会不会遇到什么麻烦?

B: 我不认为。在这个城市里有很多旅馆。看,那有一个。

A: 我们过去看一下。

（一会儿之后）

A: 你们这有空房吗?

C: 有,你们需要什么样的?

A: 我们想要一间能洗澡的标准间。

C: 我们有这样的房间。每个晚上 200 元。

A: 有没有便宜点的带我们去看看?

C: 有的。请这边走。

（一会儿之后）

A: 嘿,服务员。

D: 先生,我能帮您什么?

A: 能帮我拿条毛巾来吗?顺便说一下,可以帮我熨这件衬衫吗?

D: 没问题。

A: 非常感谢。我会在柜台那拿我的衬衫的。

D: 好的。

必备词汇　Necessary Vocabulary

stressful *adj.* 产生压力的,使紧迫的

a couple of 两个,几个

occasional *adj.* 偶然的,临时的

detailed *adj.* 详细的,逐条的

motel *n.* 汽车旅馆

laundry *n.* 要洗的衣服,洗衣店

washcloth *n.* 毛巾,面巾

terminus *n.* 终点站,终点

strenuous *adj.* 紧张的,尽心发奋的

with open arms 热情地,友好地

Business Visit 业务拜访

　　商务访问是业务、商贸关系发展的一个重要环节。当然要在事先约定好的情况下进行拜访,这样可以提高效率,以免在没有预约的情况下见不到要拜访的人。若有紧急事情也可以直接登门造访,但切不可冒昧,要以礼拜访。

基本句型 Sentence Patterns

I'm... I'd like to speak to...

我是……,我想找……

We are here to see...

我们到这要见……

I have an appointment with...

我和……有约。

I have got an appointment with...

我已经和……约好了。

I'd like to see the person in charge of ...

我想见一下负责……的人。

We specialize in ...

我们专营……

I am from...., and I was wonder if you would be interested in our products.

我来自……,不知您是否对我们的产品感兴趣。

Here is my card. I am...

这是我的名片。我是……

I wonder if you have time to ...

我想知道您是否有时间……

I have come to discuss with you ...

我来是和你们讨论……

Could do tell me how to get to ... 's office?

请问……的办公室怎么走?

I'm pleased to be here to talk about ...

我很高兴到这里同您谈……

eHow 星级典句 Classical Sentences

Will he be in the office this afternoon?

下午他会在公司吗？

Could you help me prepare some material?

你能帮我准备一些材料吗？

May I expect you at 9?

我九点钟等你好吗？

We have the appointment.

我们预约过了。

I am so pleased to see you here.

真高兴在这见到您。

Let's get down to business.

让我们言归正传。

This time I am here to show you our newest product. It will help build up your business.

这次我来是为了展示我们的最新产品，它会有助于您扩大生意。

Thank you for all of your help in this.

谢谢您的帮忙。

Thank you for doing so much for us.

谢谢您为我们做了这么多事情。

Please be my guest next time when you come to China.

下次来中国，请让我做东。

I hope I will have a chance to invite you to Beijing opera.

我希望有机会请你去看一场京剧。

Sorry, I am a little early. I hope it is not inconvenient.

对不起,我早到了一会儿,希望没有妨碍您。

It is good of you to spare the time.

您能匀出时间来真是太感谢了。

eHTw 回应方式 Repartee

Do you have an appointment?

你们有预约吗?

Take a seat, I will let him know you are here.

请稍坐一会,我去告诉他你们来了。

Please take a seat over there, and I will see whether he is available.

请您稍坐片刻,我看他现在是否可以见您。

Sorry, Mr. Green can't see you now.

对不起,格林先生现在不能见您。

Sorry to keep you waiting. I was rather tied up just now.

对不起,让您久等了,我刚才太忙了。

Would you like a cup of tea?

来杯茶吗?

You found us without too much difficulty, then?

我们的位置不太难找吧?

It's kind of you to come all this way. I hope we will tie up to. . .

你一路赶来真是太好了。希望我们能就……达成一致。

I have a little time to spare.

我只能抽出一点时间来。

eHow 情景对话 Situational Dialogue

Part 1

A: Excuse me?

B: Yes. What can I do for you?

A: Could you tell me how to get to the general manager's office?

B: Yes. Just take the stairs down to the 3 floor and turn right. You will find it on your left.

A: Thank you very much.

B: It's my pleasure.

Part 2

A: Hello. I'd like to see the person in charge of selling.

B: Mr. John? Do you have an appointment with him?

A: No. But I will take only a few minutes of his time.

B: Can I have your name, please?

A: Yes. I am Jane. Here is my business card.

B: I am sorry, but may I know what you wish to see him about?

A: Well, I come from ABC Equipment Company and I wonder if he would be interested in our products.

B: Oh. I see. Wait a moment, please, take a seat over there, and I will see whether he is available.

A: Thank you.

   (a moment later)

B: This way please.

C: Hello, Miss Jane. But I have a little time to spare.

A: I understand you are a busy man, Mr. John. It is good of you to spare the time. And I won't take you up long time. We specialize in electronic equipments. I will just show you our new products' pattern.

Part 3

A: Hello. I've got an appointment with Mr. John at 10: 00.

B: May I have your name, please?

A: Here is my business card. I am from East Textile Company.

B: Oh, he is expecting you. This way, please.

C: I have been looking forward to meeting you.

A: Nice to meet you.

C: Sorry to keep you waiting. I was rather tied up just now.

A: I am a little early. I hope it is not inconvenient.

C: No. Would you like a cup of tea?

A: Thank you. Let's get down to business. I have come to discuss with you about our deal.

C: OK. Have you take your company's sample here?

A: Yes. This time I am just here to show you our newest product. It will help build up your business.

C: When could I see the sample?

A: You can have a look at them now.

C: Let's go.

A: OK.

译文

Part 1

A: 对不起打扰您一下。

B: 怎么了,有什么能帮您的吗?

A: 你能告诉我总经理的办公室怎么走吗?

B: 是的,从这个楼梯下楼到 3 层然后朝右走,你会在你的左手边找到它。

A: 非常感谢。

B: 我很荣幸。

Part 2

A: 你好,我想见一下主管销售的人。

B: 约翰先生? 你和他有预约吗?

A: 没有,但是我只占用他几分钟时间。

B: 请问尊姓大名?

A: 好的。我叫珍妮。这是我的名片。

B: 对不起,但是请问您见他有什么事情吗?

A: 嗯,我来自 ABC 设备公司,我想知道他是否对我们的产品感兴趣。

B: 哦,我明白了。请稍等,在那边先坐一会儿,我去看看他是否有时间见您。

A: 谢谢。

（一会儿之后）

B: 这边请。

C: 你好,珍妮小姐。但是我只能抽出一点时间出来。

A: 我知道您是个大忙人,约翰先生。您能抽出时间来真是太感谢了。我不会占用您很长时间的。我们专营电子设备,我只是给您看一下我们新产品的图样。

Part 3

A: 你好,我和约翰先生在 10 点有个预约。

B: 请问尊姓大名?

A: 这是我的名片。我来自东方纺织品公司。

B: 哦,他正在等着你。这边请。

C: 我一直期望见到您。

A: 见到您很高兴。

C: 非常抱歉让您久等。我刚才真是太忙了。

A: 我来得早了一点。希望没有打扰您。

C: 没有。来一杯茶好吗?

A: 谢谢。让我们言归正传吧。我来是和你讨论我们的生意的。

C: 好的。你把你们公司产品的样品带来了没有?

A: 带来了。这次我来就是为了给您看一下我们的新产品的。它有助于扩大您的生意。

C: 我什么时候能看看样品?

A: 您现在就可以去看一看。

C: 走,去看看。

A: 好的。

必备词汇 Necessary Vocabulary

in charge of 负责,照顾,经营

specialize v. 专攻,专门研究

specialize in 擅长于,专攻

get down to 开始认真考虑

build up 增进,增大,树立

inconvenient *adj.* 不便的，有困难的

tie up 占用，密切联系，合伙

general manager 总经理

electronic *adj.* 电子的

pattern *n.* 样品，图样

textile *n.* 纺织品

sample *n.* 样品，标本，例子

In the Bank 在银行

　　从事商务活动是避免不了要与银行打交道的，能得心应手地办理各种业务对于商务活动是大有裨益的。

eHow 基本句型 Sentence Patterns

I want to change ... into RMB.

我想要把……兑换成人民币。

Could you direct me to where you change foreign money?

你能带我到兑换外币的地方吗?

Where can I send money to...

我可以在哪里汇钱到……

Where is the...

……在哪里?

I want to send some money to...

我想汇一些钱到……

What's the rate of exchange for ... into RMB today?

今天……兑换人民币的汇率是多少?

I want to have some greenbacks changed into RMB.

我想把一些美金换成人民币。

eHow 星级典句 Classical Sentences

Can you change these traveler's cheques into RMB?

你可以把这些旅行支票换成人民币吗?

Could you split this one hundred yuan note?

你能把这张百元钞换开吗?

Shall I split this one hundred note into small ones?

我能把这张百元钞票换成零钱吗?

I'm expecting some remittance from London. Have it arrived?

我在等一笔从伦敦寄过来的汇款。寄来了吗?

I'd like you to make a fifty dollar cheque payable in New York.

我想要你开一张纽约银行的 50 美元的支票。

Can you cash this cheque?

你可以兑现这张支票吗？

Can I open an account with you?

我可以在你们银行开一个账户吗？

I want to open an account and deposit some money.

我要开个账户，存一些钱。

I want to withdraw two hundred thousand yuan from my account.

我要从我的账户提取 20 万元人民币。

I should like to open a current account.

我想开一个活期存款账户。

We'd like to know how we open a checking-savings account.

我们想知道如何开一个支票储蓄账户。

I have a checking account here.

我在这里有一个支票存款账户。

I think I'd like a deposit account.

我想要开个定期存款账户。

Could you tell me the difference between a savings account and a checking account?

请告诉我储蓄存款与支票存款的区别好吗？

Please tell me the procedure for opening a savings account.

请告诉我开个储蓄账户需要什么手续。

I want to deposit my paycheck.

我想存入我的工资支票。

I'd like to draw 100 yuan against this letter of credit.

我想从这份信用证上提款 100 元。

May I draw money against the letter of credit here?

我可以在这儿用信用证取钱吗？

Could you tell me my balance?

能否把存款结余金额告诉我？

Please let me know my balance.

请告诉我结余金额。

What's the interest rate for the savings account?

储蓄存款的利率是多少？

Do you pay interest on this account?

这种存款付给利息吗？

Please tell me what the annual interest rate is.

请告诉我年利率是多少。

What's your selling rate for RMB yuan in notes today?

你们今天人民币现钞的售价是多少？

What rate are you giving?

你们提供的兑换率是多少？

What's the exchange rate today?

今天的兑换率是多少？

eHow 情景对话 Situational Dialogue

Part 1

A: May I help you?

B: Yes, I want to change some dollars into RMB. Could you direct me to where you change foreign money?

A: That's handled over here. Please follow me.

B: Thank you. By the way, where can I send money to America?

A: Please go to the Foreign Remittance section. It is counter number five. You can't miss it.

B: Thank you again.

Part 2

A: Good morning, sir. What can I do for you?

B: My name is John. Bush. I am expecting a thousand pound remittance from London. Has is arrived?

A: One moment, please. While I check our records.

(a moment later)

A: Mr. Bush!

B: Yes.

A: Your money has arrived.

B: It's good.

A: How would you like to have it?

B: Can I have it partly in RMB and partly in dollar?

A: Certainly.

B: I want to have 500 pounds in RMB and 500 pounds in dollars.

A: Both in cash?

B: No, RMB in cash, but I want the dollars in travelers cheques.

A: No problem. Would you like the commission deducted from this
thousand pounds or would you rather pay it separately?

B: You can deduct it from the remittance.

Part 3

A: Good morning, sir. Can I help you?

B: Good morning. I want to withdraw two hundred thousand dollars
from my account. This is my cheque.

A: OK, is there any request?

B: Yes. I want to have these greenbacks changed into RMB. What's the rate of exchange for dollar into RMB today?

A: One dollar exchanges 8. 20yuan.

B: Is the exchange rate fixed?

A: No. It is fluctuant.

B: Is it different in one day?

A: No. it has been decided before a working day begins in the morning.

B: Oh, I see.

A: Here you are. There are one million and sixty four thousand dollars yuan.

B: Thank you.

Part 4

A: Hello, sir. What can I do for you?

B: Could you split this one hundred yuan note?

A: Certainly, into tens?

B: Fifty in fifty yuan note and fifty in ten yuan notes, please.

A: Very well, sir. Here you are.

B: Thank you.

A: Need other helps?

B: Yes. I want to open an account and deposit some money. What kind of accounts are there?

A: There are current accounts, and fixed time deposit accounts.

B: What about interests on these accounts? I am interested in fixed time deposits accounts.

A: There are five kinds of fixed deposits. One month, three month, six month and twelve month, two year deposits.

B: Oh. I am interested in a twelve month deposit. I want to deposit 10,000 yuan.

A: For the fixed deposit please fill in this signature card.

B: OK. Where shall I sign? Here?

A: Yes. On that line. And please print your full name under it.

B: Here you are. Is that all right?

A: Yes, every thing is in order. Here you are. The certification of your twelve fixed deposit for RMB 10,000yuan.

B: Thank you.

译文

Part 1

A: 能为您效劳吗?

B: 是的,我想把一些美元兑换成人民币。你能带我到兑换外币的地方吗?

A: 在这里换,请跟我来。

B: 谢谢。顺便问一下,我可以在哪里汇钱到美国?

A: 请到国外汇款科。在 5 号窗口,您不可能会错过。

Part 2

A: 早上好,先生。我有什么能帮您的吗?

B: 我叫约翰·布什。我在等一笔从伦敦寄来的 1000 英镑的汇款。寄来了吗?

A: 请稍等一会。让我查查看。

(一会儿之后)

A: 布什先生。

B: 是的。

A：您的钱已经到了。

B：真是太好了。

A：您想怎样取呢？

B：我可以取一部分人民币一部分美元吗？

A：当然可以。

B：我想要 500 英镑的人民币和 500 英镑的美元。

A：都要现金吗？

B：不。人民币要现金，但美元要旅行支票。

A：没有问题。您要从这 1000 英镑中扣手续费，还是另外分开付手续费？

B：你可以从汇款中扣除。

Part 3

A：早上好，先生。我能帮什么吗？

B：早上好。我想从我的账户里面取 20 万美元。这是我的支票。

A：好的，还有别的要求吗？

B：是的。我想把这些美金换成人民币。今天美金兑换人民币的比率是多少？

A：一美元兑换 8.2 元人民币。

B：汇率是固定的吗？

A：不是的。它是波动的。

B：在一天之内它也可能不同吗？

A：不。在早上每个工作日开始之前就已经定下来了。

B：哦，我明白了。

A：给你。这是 164 万元人民币。

B：谢谢。

Part 4

A：先生，您好。能为您效劳吗？

B: 你能把这百元钞换开吗?

A: 当然可以,都换成 10 元的?

B: 一张 50 元的和五张 10 元的。

A: 好的,先生。给你。

B: 谢谢。

A: 还需要其他的帮助吗?

B: 是的。我想开个账户然后存一些钱。有哪几种账户?

A: 有活期存款和定期存款。

B: 这些账户的利息怎么样呢? 我对定期存款感兴趣。

A: 有五种定期存款。一个月、三个月、六个月及一年、二年的共五种。

B: 哦。我对一年期的定期存款感兴趣。我想把 10000 元存成定期的。

A: 定期存款请填这张签名卡。

B: 好的。我要签在哪? 是这儿吗?

A: 是的,那条线。请在线下面用印刷体写您的全名。

B: 给你。可以了吗?

A: 是的。一切都合规格了。给您,这是 10000 元一年期定期存款的证明书。

B: 谢谢你。

必备词汇 　Necessary Vocabulary

greenback *n.* 美钞,背部为绿色之动物

cheque *n.* 支票

split *v.* 分裂,分离

remittance *n.* 汇款,汇寄之款

payable *adj.* 可付的,应付的

deposit *v.* 存款,存放物

withdraw *v.* 收回,撤出

credit *n.* 信用,银行存款

savings account 储蓄存款账户

annual *n.* 一年一次的,每年的

deduct from 扣除

certification *n.* 证明

Chapter 4   Dealing Process

Chapter 4   Dealing Process

Attending fair 参加交易会

无论是购买商品还是出售商品，交易会都提供了一个良好的平台，充分地利用交易会或者可以使你的产品成功销售并威名远播，或者你能在那购买到价格适当的、最新的产品。

eH W 基本句型　Sentence Patterns

May I help you?

有什么能帮您的吗？

I am interested in your range of. . .

我对你们……系列感兴趣。

How about the prices?

价格如何？

We can deliver the goods within. . . days upon receipt of your order.

自收到订单之日起……天内交货。

Would you like a copy of brochure?

这是我们产品的说明书，要一份吗？

What's the price difference?

价格有何差异？

Would you like a brochure?

请问要一份产品小册子吗？

Let me show you our. . .

让我向您展示我们的……

Let me show you our stand.

让我向您展示我们的陈列台。

Perhaps you would be interested in our. . .

也许您会对我们的……感兴趣。

eHow 星级典句 Classical Sentences

Do you like our products?

您喜欢我们的产品吗？

Have you seen our latest innovation?

你见过我们最新的产品吗？

This is our newly developed product. Would you like to see it?

这是我们新开发的产品。您要不要看一看？

Let me show you how to operate the machine.

让我为您示范这部机器的操作方法。

This is our company's address and telephone number. If you have any questions, don't hesitate to contact us.

这是我们公司的联络地址和电话，如有任何问题，请不要客气，尽快与我们联系。

Please write down your name and the products you want to order on this order sheet.

请在这份订单上填写您的姓名和订购的产品。

We've got some new models here.

我们这里有一些新产品的样品。

They are all available from stock.

全部都有现货供应。

Can you give me a good discount on a large order?

大宗订货有优惠折扣吗？

Would you like to meet our sales representative?

你是否想见一下我们的销售代表？

It's only been on the market for a couple of months.

这种产品才上市一两个月。

I'll get a set of illustrations for you.

我去拿套样品给你。

This is our showroom. Quite a few overseas buyers have visited it before.

这是我们的陈列室，有很多外国客户到这里参观过。

Here are the most favorite products on display.

这里展出的是最受欢迎的产品。

This is our newly developed product. Would you like to see it?

这是我们新开发的产品，您要不要看一看？

情景对话　Situational Dialogue

Part 1

A: Good morning, may I help you?

B: Yes. I am interested in your range of electric bicycles.

A: Here are the most favorite products on display.

B: Could you show me something about them?

A: Would you like a copy of brochure? And I will tell you some things about them in the meantime.

B: Thank you.

A: The electric bicycles manufactured in our company are famous all over the country. The bicycles on your right consume less electricity than former types when they run the same distance. On your left it is designed specially for women. You can find it is smart and pretty.

B: Very good. Are they all available from stock?

A: Yes, certainly.

B: How about the price?

A: The recommended retail prices can be found on the brochure.

B: Oh. Let me have a look. It's not cheaper.

A: It deserves the price because of the good quality.

B: What about delivery time?

A: We can deliver the goods within 5 days if you order today.

B: Could you give me a discount on a large order?

A: It depends on the size of the order.

B: Oh, I see. I need to think it over.

A: This is my card. If you need the order, please call me.

B: Thank you.

Part 2

A: Hello, sir. Do you like our products?

B: No. Thanks.

A: Take your time, sir. Have you seen our latest innovation?

B: No.

A: Perhaps you would be interested in our sport sweaters. Let me show you our stand.

B: All right.

A: Would you like a brochure?

B: Thank you.

A: This way, please. This is our showroom. Quite a few overseas buyers have visited it before. Here are the most favorite products on display.

B: Wow... These sweaters are very colorful and feel nice. It's a pure wool sweater?

A: Yes. It's only been on the market for a couple of months. The fashionable styles of the sweaters on display at the fair interested the visitors very much.

B: I want to meet your sales representative.

A: I am the representative.

B: Oh. I want to order them.

A: Really? That's good.

译文

Part 1

A: 早上好,有什么能为您效劳的吗?

B: 是的。我对你们生产的电动自行车系列感兴趣。

A: 这里展出的是最受欢迎的产品。

B: 你能给我介绍一下吗?

A: 先给您一份产品说明书好吗?同时我会给你介绍我们的产品。

B: 谢谢。

A: 我们厂生产的电动自行车在全国都是有名的。在你右手边的自行车跑同样的路程比以前型号的自行车耗电量要少;在你左手边的是专门为女式设计的,你会发现它们很灵巧很漂亮。

B: 非常好。全部都有现货供应吗?

A: 是的,当然了。

B: 价格如何?

A: 在那个小册子上有建议零售价。

B: 哦。让我看一下。并不便宜。

A: 质量好,物有所值。

B: 什么时候能交货呢?

A: 如果你今天下订单的话我们五天之内就可以交货。

B: 大宗订货有优惠折扣吗?

A: 这要看订单的大小了。

B: 哦,我明白了。我需要仔细考虑一下。

A: 这是我的名片。如果你要下订单,请给我打电话。

B: 谢谢你。

Part 2

A: 您好,先生。您喜欢我们的产品吗?

B: 不了。谢谢。

A: 别着急啊,先生。您看过我们的最新产品了吗?

B: 没有。

A: 或许你对我们的运动衫感兴趣。让我向您展示我们的陈列台。

B: 好吧。

A: 您要不要先看个小册子?

B: 谢谢。

A: 这边请。这是我们的陈列室,有很多外国客户到这儿参观过。这里展出的是最受欢迎的产品。

B: 哇……这些运动衫颜色很丰富,手感也很好。它们是纯羊毛的吗?

A: 是的。这种产品才上市一两个月。展销会上展出的时尚的运动衫非常吸引顾客。

B: 我想要见你们的销售代表。

A: 我就是销售代表。

B: 哦。我想订这些运动衫。

A: 真的吗?那真是太好了。

必备词汇　Necessary Vocabulary

receipt　*n.*　收条,收据

stand　*n.*　台,看台,架子

innovation　*n.*　改革,创新

discount　*n.*　折扣

representative　*n. / adj.*　代表,典型的,有代表性的

illustration　*n.*　例子,图表

showroom　*n.*　(商品、样品的)陈列室

in range of　在……范围之内

manufacture　*v.*　制造,加工

consume　*v.*　消耗,消费

retail price　零售价

deserve　*v.*　应受,值得

fashionable　*adj.*　流行的,时髦的

Inquiry 询价

询价是买卖双方进入实质性磋商阶段的关键一步。为了抓住买家，在交谈技巧上最好渐进式介绍一下产品情况与交易达成的条件，努力使双方在感情上拉近距离，最后让对方的购买欲望变成购买行动。询价包括询问商品样式、商品价格、折扣情况以及交货情况等。

eHow 基本句型 Sentence Patterns

Can I have a look at the pattern books first?

我能否先看一下样本？

Can you make delivery within. . .

你们能在……以内交货吗？

How much of a discount would you allow us on. . .

在……方面你们能给多少折扣？

We are in great need of. . .

我们需要一大批……

Could you give me some ideas about your prices?

请你介绍一下你方的价格好吗？

Could you give me an indication of price?

能否谈谈价格方面的情况呢？

Thank you for your detailed information.

谢谢你提供详情。

——以上适合于买方

Here is the price list.

这是价格单。

Our offer holds good until. . .

我们报盘有效期至……

Thank you for your inquiry.

谢谢您的询价。

——以上适合于卖方

eH💡w 星级典句 Classical Sentences

I would like to have your illustrated catalogue so that I can study it more carefully.

我想要一份带说明书的目录以便我再仔细研究一下。

We hope you will give us some special discounts.

我希望你们能够给我们一些优惠折扣。

We want to know how long it will take you to deliver the goods.

我们很想知道你们交货时间有多长。

You'll have to reconsider the price.

贵方得重新考虑一下价格。

I have seen your samples and studied your catalogues, and I think they will find a ready market in Beijing.

我已经看过你们的样品和商品目录，我觉得这些商品在北京会很有市场的。

How long does it take you to make a delivery?

你方通常需要多长时间交货？

I will place a larger order this time, if the price is more favorable.

如果价格更优惠一点的话,这次我的订货量将更大。

Please quote us as soon as you receive our inquiry.

一收到咨询信,请尽快报价。

We can't accept your offer. Your price is too high.

我们不能接受贵方的报价。你们的价格太高了。

We have learned from our agent the scope of your business activities.

我们已经从代理商处得知贵公司的经营范围。

——以上适合于买方

Here are our brochures and relevant publicity materials which may

必备词汇 Necessary Vocabulary

inquiry *n.* 咨询,调查

catalogue *n.* 目录

special discount 特别折扣

reconsider *v.* 重新考虑,重新审议

favorable *adj.* 良好的,讨人喜欢的

quote *v.* 引用,引证

publicity *n.* 公开

wise *adj.* 明智的,聪明的

reputation *n.* 名誉,名声

cooperation *n.* 合作,协作

mutual benefit 互惠,互利

Bargining 讨价还价

　　讨价还价是交易往来中最重要的一个环节，关系到企业切身的利润，讨价还价的关键不在于使对方哑口无言，而是要使其心悦诚服。

eHow 基本句型   Sentence Patterns

We would be interested to sign contract for. . .

我们有意……签这份合同。

We are in tough position. It would be a great help if you could reduce the unit cost by. . .

我们的处境困难。如果你们能把单价……的话,会帮上很大的忙。

We may suggest that you reduce your price by. . .That would help you to introduce your goods to our customers.

我们建议你方降价……,这将有助于把你方商品介绍给我方客户。

Our compromise proposal is based on. . .

我们的折衷意见是……

Your offer sounds good, but. . .

您的报价听起来不错,但……

What's the best price you're prepared to offer for your product?

你们的产品最优惠的价格是多少呢?

——以上适合于买方

If your order is large enough, we will consider reducing our prices by. . .

如果订单大,我们可以考虑减价……

Let's compromise.

让我们还是各退一步吧。

I'm sure there is some room for negotiation.

我肯定还有商量的余地。

——以上适合于卖方

eH w 星级典句　Classical Sentences

Your unit price seems fair enough, but we're hoping for a higher discount rate.

单价似乎合理,但我们希望给予更高的折扣率。

I think your price is on the high side.

我认为贵方价格偏高。

Your price is too much on the high side for us to accept.

你方价格太高,我们无法接受。

Compared with what is quoted by other suppliers, your price is not competitive at all.

与其他供货商的价格相比,你们的价格毫无竞争力。

What do you think will be a fair price for your product?

你认为你们产品的价格公平吗?

I can show you other quotations that are lower than yours.

我可以拿出比你们更低的报价给你看。

If you hang on to the original offer, business is impossible.

如果你还是坚持最初的开价,我们则无法达成交易。

If we can't reach an agreement, we have to find another partner.

如果我们不能达成协议,我们只能另找伙伴了。

The price you quoted is so high that we will have to cancel this transaction.

你方价格太高,我们不得不取消这笔交易。

That's a high price! It will be difficult for us to make any sales.

价格这么高,我方很难有销路。

The market is declining. We recommend your immediate acceptance.

市场在萎缩,我们建议你方马上接受。

Since we are likely to place sizable orders regularly we hope that you will make some special concessions.

由于我方将定期大批量订购,希望贵方做出一些特殊的让步。

If you do have the sincerity to do business with us, please show me your cards and put them on the table.

如果您确有诚意与我们做生意,请摊牌吧。

Don't forget the discount.

别忘了折扣。

——以上适合于买方

There is little scope for reducing the price because our price is already set at a reasonable level.

价格下调的空间不大,我们的定价合情合理。

I can assure you the prices we offer you are very favorable.

我敢保证我们向你提供的价位是合理的。

If you take quality into consideration, you will find our price reasonable.

如果您把质量考虑进去的话,您会发现我方价格是合理的。

This is our minimum price. We can't make any further concessions.

这是我方的最低价格,不能再让了。

I hope we can conclude the transaction at this price.

希望我们能就此价格达成交易。

The price of this commodity has recently been adjusted due to advance in cost.

由于成本上升,货物价格近来已做调整。

It's regrettable that your order has been dropped owing to no agreement in price.

非常遗憾,由于价格上无法达成协议,此项订单无法实施。

I'm sorry that the difference between our price and your counter offer is too wide. It's impossible for us to entertain your counter offer.

很遗憾,我方的价格与你方的还盘差距还是太大。我们不可能接受。

I'm afraid that we can't make any further reduction on the price, which would other wise leave us a much lower margin.

恐怕再进一步降低价格的话,我们的赚头就相当小了。

According to the quantity you wish to order, we may adjust our prices accordingly.

根据你们要订的数量的多少,我们会对价格做相应的调整。

——以上适合于卖方

eHow 情景对话 Situational Dialogue

Part 1

A: I have seen your price list. And I think your price is on the high side.

B: No, no, no. I can assure you the prices we offer you are very favorable.

A: Really? I can show you other quotations that are lower than yours. Compared with what is quoted by other suppliers, your price is not competitive at all.

B: Maybe. But if you take quality into consideration, you will find our price reasonable. Our products are famed all over the world. Maybe other companies would quote lower price, but I am sure the quality is different.

A: That's a high price! It will be difficult for us to make any sales.

B: So far as the price is concerned, it is workable.

A: Since we are likely to place sizable orders regularly we hope that you will make some special concessions.

B: I'm afraid that we can't make any further reduction on the price, which would other wise leave us a much lower margin.

A: If you hang on to the original offer, business is impossible.

B: It's regrettable. But this is our minimum price. We can't make any further concessions.

Part 2

A: Hello, Mr. John. I am glad to see you again.

B: Nice to meet you. I come to have a look at your products.

A: Do you have any need?

B: Yes. I am interested in your sweaters. Could you give me a brochure and a price list?

A: Yes. Here you are.

B: Oh. I find that your price is 20% higher than that of last year.

A: You may notice that the cost of raw materials has gone up in recent years.

B: It must be rather difficult for us to push any sales if we buy it at this price.

A: When you compare the prices, you must take everything into consideration. For instance, quality, delivery, after-sales service, etc. No matter how high the price is, we are sure you can put it in your market.

B: To conclude the business, you need to cut your price at least by 10%, I believe.

A: A discount of six percent is all that I'm authorized to offer you.

B: All right.

译文

Part 1

A: 我已经看过你们的价格单了。并且我认为贵方产品价格偏高。

B: 不,不,不。我能保证我们所提供的价格是非常合理的。

A: 真的吗？我可以拿出比你们更低的报价给你看。与其他供货商的价格相比,你们的价格毫无竞争力。

B: 或许。但是如果你把我们的质量考虑进去的话,你会发现我们的价格合情合理。我们的产品是享誉世界的。或许其他厂商会给你更低的价格,但是我确信质量是不同的。

A: 价格这么高,我方很难有销路。

B: 就价格而言,是做得开的。

A: 由于我方将定期大批量订购,希望贵方做出一些特殊的让步。

B: 恐怕再进一步降低价格的话,我们的赚头就相当小了。

A: 如果你还是坚持最初的开价,我们则无法达成交易。

B: 非常遗憾。但是这已经是我们能给的最低价了,不能再做出任何让步了。

Part 2

A: 你好,约翰先生。很高兴再次见到你。

B: 见到你很高兴。我来看一下你们的产品。

A: 你有什么需要吗?

B: 是的。我对你们的毛线衫很感兴趣。能给我个小册子和一份价格单看看吗?

A: 好的。给你。

B: 哦。我发现你们的价格比去年高了 20%。

A: 您可能注意到了近年来原材料的价格上涨了。

B: 如果我们按这个价格购买,将很能难推销。

A: 当你在考虑对比价格时,必须把一切都要考虑进去。比如质量、交货期、售后服务等等。不管价格多高,我们肯定你方能在贵方市场售出。

B: 我认为要做成这笔交易,您至少要降价 10%。

A: 6% 的折扣是我权限内所能给你的。

B: 好吧。

必备词汇　Necessary Vocabulary

contract *n.* 合同,契约

unit cost 单价,单位成本

compromise *n.* 妥协,折衷

proposal *n.* 提议,建议

negotiation *n.* 商议,谈判

on the high side (价格)偏高

competitive *adj.* 竞争的

fair price 公平价格

hang on to 紧紧握住

declining *adj.* 倾斜的,衰退中的

concession *n.* 让步

sincerity *n.* 诚挚,真诚

take into consideration 考虑到

minimum price 最低价

regrettable *adj.* 可叹的,可惜的

owing to 由于,因……之缘故

margin *n.* 利润

Order and Delivery 订货与交货

　　订货是买卖双方交易的实质性进展，卖方应尽量满足买方的订货要求、产品样式、数量，这样才能使合作关系长期保持下去；而交货则体现了卖方的商务能力，能否尽快、按时交货关系到买方的切身利益、产品销路。

eHow 基本句型　Sentence Patterns

Can you supply. . .

你们能供应……吗？

I have decided to place an order for. . .

我已经决定订购……

I'd like to place an order. . .

我想要预定……

Could you expect an earlier shipment by. . .

你们能否在……之前早一点发货？

The time of delivery is very important to us.

交货时间对我们来说非常重要。

Let's discuss the delivery date first.

让我们首先讨论一下交货日期。

——以上适合于买方

We have to postpone the shipment because. . .

因为……我们必须延迟装运的时间。

It was a pleasure to receive your recent order.

十分高兴接到你方的最新订单。

I am glad to tell you personally how much I appreciate your order.

我很高兴告诉你，非常高兴你方的订货。

——以上适合于卖方

When can we expect delivery if we order now?

如果我们现在订货,你们何时能交货呢?

Please quote your prices, including packing and delivery to our warehouse.

请报你方价格,包括包装及送货到我方仓库的费用。

We want the goods in our market at the earliest possible date.

我们想把商品尽早投放市场。

We would be most grateful if you could send the goods as soon as possible for these goods are urgently needed.

由于我们急需这批货,如能尽快发货,将不胜感激。

We want to cancel the contract because of your delay in delivery.

由于贵方交货拖延,我方要求取消合同。

The buyer has the right to cancel the contract unilaterally if the seller fails to ship the goods within the L/C validity.

如果卖方不能在信用证有效期内交货的话,买方有权单方面取消合同。

——以上适合于买方

We assure you of a punctual execution of your order.

我们一定准时执行你方订单。

We'll ship our goods in accordance with the terms of the contract.

我们将按合同条款交货。

I am pleased to say that we will be able to deliver the transport facilities you require.

很高兴告诉您你方要求的运输设备我方可以发货。

We have a lot of orders to fill.

我们要完成大量的订单。

That item is out of stock at the moment.

这种货品暂时缺货。

We're sorry that the said goods are not available from stock.

很抱歉所述货物没有存货。

While thanking you for your order, we have to explain that the supplies of raw materials are difficult to obtain and we have no choose but to decline your order.

非常感谢你的订单,但由于原材料供应不足,我们不得不拒绝你们的订货。

We are sorry that we are not presently in a position to deliver your order as requested because our entire production capacity has already been committed for this month.

由于我方这个月的生产任务都已安排满了,所以很难在贵公司要求的交货日期交货。

We have difficulties in arranging shipping.

我们安排海运有困难。

Delivery has to be put off due to the strike of the workers at the port.

由于港口工人罢工,交货只好推迟。

——以上适合于卖方

情景对话 Situational Dialogue

Part 1

A: I have decided to place an order for your toys.

B: It was a pleasure to receive your recent order.

A: Let's discuss the delivery date first.

B: You will expect the delivery within 10 days upon your order.

A: Very good. The time of delivery is very important to us.

B: Don't worry. We assure you of a punctual execution of your order.

Part 2

A: I'd like to place an order of your machines.

B: I am glad to tell you personally how much I appreciate your order.

A: When can we expect delivery if we order now?

B: We will deliver as soon as possible.

A: Could you expect an earlier shipment by October? We want the goods in our market at the earliest possible date.

B: We have a lot of orders to fill. I am not sure if we will finish by October.

A: We would be most grateful if you could send the goods as soon as possible for these goods are urgently needed.

B: Take it easy. We will make our great efforts to do.

A: Thank you very much.

Part 3

A: Have you received our order?

B: Yes. But we're sorry that the said goods are not available from stock.

A: We are not so urgent need. Could you deliver at the last of this month?

B: While thanking you for your order, we have to explain that the supplies of raw materials are difficult to obtain and we have no choose but to decline your order.

A: Oh, thank you. I have to ask other manufacturer.

B: It's regrettable. But I hope we will have the chance of cooperation in future.

A: Me too.

Part 4

A: I am sorry to tell you we can't deliver your goods on time.

B: What?

A: We have difficulties in arranging shipping.

B: What difficulties?

A: Delivery has to be put off due to the strike of the workers at the port.

B: But the deliver date is very important for us. If we could not put them in the market in time while other corporations sell up their goods, we will be out of pocket. Do you have any other method to deliver the goods?

A: I am sorry.

B: We want to cancel the contract because of your delay in delivery.

A: How you can?

B: The buyer has the right to cancel the contract unilaterally if the seller fails to ship the goods within the L/C validity.

译文

Part 1

A: 我已经决定要订一批你们的玩具。

B: 非常高兴接到您的新订单。

A: 让我们首先讨论一下交货日期吧。

B: 你能在你下订单 10 天之内收到货物。

A: 非常好。交货时间对我们来说太重要了。

B: 不要担心。我方一定准时执行你方订单。

Part 2

A: 我想要订一批你们的机器。

B: 我很高兴告诉您我是多么感激您的订货。

A: 如果我们现在订货你们会在什么时候交货呢?

B: 我们会尽快交货的。

A: 你们能在 10 月到来之前尽早交货吗? 我们想让这些货物尽早投放市场。

B: 我们有很多订单要完成。我不能确定我们能否在 10 月前完成。

A: 由于我们急需这批货,如能尽快发货,将不胜感激。

B: 别担心。我们会尽最大努力的。

A: 非常感谢。

Part 3

A: 你们收到我们的订单了吗?

B: 是的。但是很抱歉,这种货物我们现在没有存货。

A: 我们不是很着急。你们能在这个月底交货吗?

B: 非常感谢你的订单,但由于原材料供应不足,我们不得不拒绝你们的订货。

A: 哦,谢谢。我得找其他厂商问问。

B: 非常遗憾。我希望我们将来能有合作的机会。

A: 我也是。

Part 4

A: 非常抱歉告诉您,我们不能按时交货了。

B: 什么?

A: 我们在安排海运上有困难。

B: 什么困难?

A: 由于港口工人罢工,交货只好推迟。

B: 但是交货日期对我们来说太重要了。如果我们不能及时把货
物投放市场而其他公司把货物卖光的话,我们就得赔钱了。
你们有没有别的办法来运输货物?

A: 非常抱歉。

B: 由于贵方交货拖延,我方要求取消合同。

A: 你们怎么能取消呢?

B: 如果卖方不能在信用证有效期内交货的话,买方有权单方面
取消合同。

必备词汇　Necessary Vocabulary

shipment *n.* 装船,出货

personally *adv.* 亲自

warehouse *n.* 仓库,货栈

unilateral *adj.* 单方面的,单边的

punctual *adj.* 严守时刻的,准时的

execution *n.* 实行,执行

in accordance with 与……一致,依照

raw *adj.* 未加工的

capacity *n.* 容量,生产量

put off 推迟,拖延

urgent need 急需的

Payment 付款

付款这一过程在整个交易过程中是最重要的，因为只有这个过程才显示出了商品流通的真正目的，即资本流通。多样化的付款方式可以方便您的交易，诚信可靠的银行选择可以使客户放心，交易顺利。

eHiw 基本句型 Sentence Patterns

We generally accept payment by collection, but other modes of payment, such as. . .

我们基本上采用托收支付方式,但也有其他支付方式,例如……

In view of the long period of trading we have enjoyed with your company we are prepared to allow you a further. . .days.

考虑到我们之间长期的贸易关系,我们同意你方延期……天付款的要求。

We will expect your payment not later than. . .Otherwise we'll put the matter into the hands of our solicitor.

你方支付不得迟于……,否则我们将交于律师处理该事宜。

We only accept payment by. . .

我们只接受……付款方式。

Would it be possible for you to make an exception and accept. . .

你们能不能破例接受……付款方式?

Payment should be made by. . .

要凭……支付。

eHiw 星级典句 Classical Sentences

Shall we talk about the terms of payment?

我们是否来谈谈付款的问题?

We will make payment without delay.

我们将准时付款。

The question of payment will take top priority in our discussions.

就支付问题我们将优先讨论。

Your prompt payment would be greatly appreciated.

你们立即付款我们将感激不尽。

We are accustomed to sales against L/C available by draft at sight.

我们习惯于按即期汇票信用证出售货物。

Please open your L/C immediately to facilitate our shipping arrangement.

请即开信用证，以便我们安排装船。

In view of the small quantity of the order, we propose payment by D/P with collection through a bank so as to simplify the payment procedure.

由于这批订货量不大，建议付款方式采用付款交单银行托收，以便简化手续。

In view of our long friendly relations and the efforts you have made in pushing the sales, we agree to change the terms of payment from L/C at sight to D/P at sight, however, this should not be taken as a precedent.

鉴于我们长期的友好关系和您在推销方面做出的努力，我们同意将即期信用证付款方式改为即期付款交单，但下不为例。

eHow 情景对话 Situational Dialogue

Part 1

A: The question of payment will take top priority in our discussions.

B: Yes. What is your usual practice of payment?

A: We only accept payment by D/A.

B: Would it be possible for you to make an exception and accept payment by irrevocable Letter of Credit?

A: As request for D/A at sight is our customary practice which we must adhere to, we hope that you will not regard it as being unaccommodating.

B: All right.

Part 2

A: Shall we talk about the terms of payment?

B: OK. We are trying for the bank's loan.

A: Your prompt payment would be greatly appreciated.

B: But I think the payment date will be put off for uncertain days.

A: In view of the long period of trading we have enjoyed with your company we are prepared to allow you a further 20 days.

B: 20 days? Is there any further free time?

A: No. We will expect your payment not later than September 30. Otherwise we'll put the matter into the hands of our solicitor.

B: All right. We will pay as soon as possible.

译文

Part 1

A: 支付问题将最优先讨论。

B: 是的。你们通常的付款方法是什么？

A: 我们只接受承兑交单。

B: 你们能不能破例接受不可撤销的跟单信用证？

A: 由于要求采用承兑交单是我方必须坚持的一贯做法，所以我们很希望贵方不要认为我方不肯通融。

B: 好吧。

Part 2

A: 让我们来谈谈付款的问题吧。

B: 好的。我们正在向银行争取贷款。

A: 你们尽快付款我们将不胜感激。

B: 但是我想我们的付款日期会无限期拖延。

A: 考虑到我们之间长期的贸易关系，我们同意你方延期 20 天付款的要求。

B: 20 天？有没有更进一步的宽限？

A: 没有。你方支付不得迟于 9 月 30 日，否则我们将交于律师处理该事宜。

B: 好吧。我们会尽快付款的。

必备词汇　Necessary Vocabulary

solicitor *n.* 律师，法律顾问

exception *n.* 除外，例外

top priority 应予最优先考虑的事

facilitate *v.* 使容易，使便利

so as to 使得，以致

simplify *v.* 简单化，单一化

precedent *n.* 先例

Transportation 货物运输

　　也许运输并没有被列入商品生产流通的过程，但是它却是商品流通中不可缺少的一个环节。在实际运输过程中仍然有很多问题需要注意，只有卖方把商品交到买方的手上，交易过程才算切实的完成了。

eH w **基本句型** Sentence Patterns

Delivery costs will have to be borne by the manufacturer, I'm afraid.

运费恐怕要由制造商来承担。

Whose responsibility is the shipment charges?

运费由谁来负责呢？

Who assumes shipment cost?

谁负担运费呢？

When could we typically expect delivery?

我们希望常规的发货时间是什么时候呢？

What sort of guarantees are there against late delivery?

对于延迟发货有什么保证呢？

Please show us the shipping costs for several possible carries.

请告诉我们几种可能的运输方式的价格。

It's essential to choose the right means of transportation.

选择合适的运输方式很重要。

It's faster but more expensive to ship goods by air.

空运较快但运费较高。

The goods will be transhipped in Hong Kong.

货物将在香港转船。

In that case, we might need to reopen the question of prices.

如果是那样，我们也许需要重新讨论价格。

eHOW 星级典句　Classical Sentences

That seems quite soon considering the nature of the product and shipping time.

考虑到产品的性质和运输时间那看来太快了。

If you can guarantee on-time delivery with a penalty for late delivery, we can accept your sales price.

如果你能保证用惩罚延误发货方式准时发货，我们可以接受你们的销售价。

We would also want you to cover insurance and the cost of transporting the goods to the port.

我们也要贵方负责保险以及把货物运到港口的费用。

To ensure faster delivery, you are asked to forward the order by air freight.

为了确保迅速交货，我方要求空运发货。

Since we need the goods urgently, we must insist on express shipment.

由于我方急需这批货物，我方坚持使用快递装运。

——以上适合于买方

Other buyers are satisfied with it, but we could delay it if you could pay 40 percent up front.

其他买主对这货物很满意，但如果你能先付40%货款，我们可以延迟交货。

That would be the responsibility of the buyer. We are prepared, however, to provide all the documentation costs.

那是属于买方的责任，我们仅承担提供所有文件的费用。

We can supply from stock and will have no trouble in meeting your delivery date.

我们可以提供现货并按你方所定日期交货。

We can offer door-to-door delivery services.

我们提供送货上门服务。

You can stay assured that shipment will be effected according to the contract stipulation.

你尽管放心，我们将按合同规定如期装船。

Generally speaking, it's cheaper but slower to ship goods by sea than by rail.

总的来说，海运比铁路运输更便宜，但速度慢一些。

Because of the type of purchase, we can only ship by road.

由于商品的性质，我方只能使用公路运输。

If the customer requests a carrier other than truck, he must bear the additional charge.

如果顾客坚持用卡车以外的运输工具，就必须负担额外费用。

There may be some quantity difference when loading the goods, but not more than 3%.

货物装船时可能会有一些数量出入，但不会超过 3%。

To make it easier for us to get the goods ready for shipment, we hope that partial shipment is allowed.

为了便于我方备货装船，希望允许分批发运。

We are sorry to delay the shipment because our manufacturer has met unexpected difficulties.

恕延期装船，因为我们厂家遇到了预料不到的困难。

——以上适合于卖方

eHⓘw 情景对话 Situational Dialogue

Part 1

A: How will you deliver the goods?

B: We will make use of shipment.

A: Whose responsibility is the shipment charges?

B: Delivery costs will have to be borne by the purchaser, I'm afraid.

A: Please show us the shipping costs.

B: Here is the price list.

A: Since we need the goods urgently, we must insist on express shipment.

B: In that case, we might need to reopen the question of prices.

A: The price is not an issue. What sort of guarantees are there against late delivery?

B: Yes. We will bear all your loss which is arose by our delay.

A: OK. I think we will have a good cooperation.

Part 2

A: Hello, Mr. John.

B: Hello, Miss. Jane.

A: Have our goods been delivered?

B: We are sorry to delay the shipment because our manufacturer has met unexpected difficulties.

A: What? The delivery date is very important for us. To ensure faster delivery, you are asked to forward the order by air freight.

B: But who assumes the added shipment cost?

A: It's certainly you.

B: We will decline the transportation cost to make up our defect. Do you agree?

A: We would also want you to cover insurance and the cost of transporting the goods to the port.

B: OK. We accept it.

Part 3

A: Could you ship our goods by train?

B: Why? According to our contract we should ship them by truck.

A: We hope we can receive the goods as soon as possible. Generally speaking, it's faster in despite of more expensive to ship goods by train than by truck.

B: Don't worry. We will have no trouble in meeting your delivery date.

A: Could you change the transportation instrument?

B: I'm sorry. If the customer requests a carrier other than truck, he must bear the additional charge.

A: Since you commit that you will deliver the goods on time, we don't insist on the changing.

B: All right. Thank you.

译文

Part 1

A: 你们怎么运送货物呢？

B: 我们会利用船运。

A: 运费由谁来承担呢？

B: 运费恐怕要由买方来承担。

A: 请告诉一下我们运输费用。

B: 这是价格单。

A: 由于我方急需这批货物，我方坚持使用快递装运。

B: 如果是那样，我们也许需要重新讨论价格。

A: 价格不是问题。对于延迟发货有什么保证呢？

B: 是的。我们会承担所有因我们延迟而给您造成的损失。

A: 好的。我想我们会合作愉快的。

Part 2

A: 你好，约翰先生。

B: 你好，珍妮小姐。

A: 我们的货物已经运了吗？

B: 非常抱歉延迟装船，因为我们厂家遇到了预料不到的困难。

A: 什么？交货日期对我们来说非常重要。为了确保迅速交货，我方要求空运发货。

B: 但是谁来承担额外的运输费用呢？

A: 当然是你方了。

B: 我们会减少运费以弥补我方过失。你们同意吗？

A: 我们也要贵方负责保险以及把货物运到港口的费用。

B: 好的。我们接受这个条件。

Part 3

A: 你们能用火车运送我们的货物吗？

B: 为什么？根据我们的合同我们应该用卡车运输。

A: 我希望我们能尽快收到那批货。总的来说,铁路运输比公路运输更快,虽然贵一些。

B: 别担心。我们能够按期交货。

A: 你们不能改变一下运输工具吗？

B: 很抱歉。如果顾客坚持用卡车以外的运输工具,就必须负担额外费用。

A: 既然你们承诺会按时交货,那我们就不再坚持更改了。

B: 好的。谢谢。

必备词汇   Necessary Vocabulary

guarantee *n.* 保证,保证书,担保

essential *adj.* 基本的,必要的

tranship *v.* 换船,换车

reopen *v.* 重开,再开始

penalty *n.* 处罚,罚款

air freight 空运发货

door-to-door 挨户访问的

stipulation *n.* 约定,约束,契约

partial *adj.* 部分的,局部的

Chapter 5   Other Affairs

Chapter 5　Other Affairs

Negotiation 谈判

在国际谈判场合要与多国人士打交道，灵活运用地道的英语对话洽谈，首次交锋便让对方知难而退，为自己及公司谋取更多利益，打场漂亮的商场舌战，顺利地完成任务。

eH●w 基本句型 \ Sentence Patterns

It will be easier for us to get down to. . .

对我们来说认真面对……很容易

We could add it to the agenda.

我们可以把它列入议程。

Let's negotiate. . .

让我们来讨论一下……

I still have some questions concerning. . .

就……方面我还有些问题要问。

Do you think there is something wrong with. . .

你认为……有问题吗?

No, I'm afraid you misunderstood me. What I was trying to say was. . .

不,恐怕你误解了。我想说的是……

We can't agree with. . .

我们无法同意……

It depends on. . .

那要视……而定。

The negotiations on. . . turned out to be very successful.

就……方面的谈判非常成功。

I hope this meeting is productive.

我希望这是一次富有成效的会谈。

We'll come out from this meeting as winners.

这次会谈的结果将是双赢的。

eHow 星级典句　Classical Sentences

They scheduled the negotiation at nine tomorrow morning.

他们把谈判时间订在明天早上 9 点。

Better have something we can get our hands on rather than just spend all our time talking.

有些实际材料拿到手会比坐着闲聊强。

Is there any way of ensuring we'll have enough time for our talks?

我们是否能保证有充足的时间来谈判?

We are ready.

我们准备好了。

I need more information.

我需要更多的信息。

We can postpone our meeting until tomorrow.

我们可以把会议延迟到明天。

That will eat up a lot of time.

那会耗费很多时间。

It will be easier for us to get down to facts then.

这样就容易进行实质性的谈判了。

How would you like to proceed with the negotiations?

你认为该怎样来进行这次谈判呢?

——以上适合于谈判准备

Would anyone like something to drink before we begin?

在我们正式开始前,大家喝点什么?

May I propose that we break for coffee now?

我可以提议休息一下,喝杯咖啡吗?

I suggest that we take a break.

建议休息一下。

Let's dismiss and return in an hour.

咱们休会,一个钟头后再回来。

We need a break.

我们需要暂停一下。

May I suggest that we continue tomorrow.

我建议明天再继续,好吗?

——以上适合于谈判礼仪

We'd have to compare notes on what we've discussed during the day.

我们想用点时间来研究讨论一下白天谈判的情况。

The longer we wait , the less likely we will come up with anything.

时间拖得越久,我们成功的机会就越少。

We have done a lot.

我们已经取得不少的进展。

——以上适合于谈判总结

Sorry, but could you kindly repeat what you just said?

抱歉,你可以重复刚刚所说的吗?

I could not catch your question. Could you repeat it, please?

我没听清楚你们的问题,你能重复一次吗?

Please say it again.

请再说一遍。

Would you speak a little louder?

请你说大声一点好吗?

Will you speak up, please?

请你大声一点好吗?

Will you speak more slowly?

请你说慢一点好吗?

——以上适合于谈判心理攻势

That's a good idea.

是个好主意。

I agree with you.

我赞成。

Oh, I'm sorry, I misunderstood you. Then I go along with you.

哦,对不起,我误解你了。那样的话,我同意你的观点。

We accept your proposal, on the condition that you order 20,000 units.

如果您订 2 万台,我们会接受您的建议。

I don't think that's a good idea.

我不认为那是个好主意。

Not in the long run.

从长远来说并不是这样。

Frankly, we can't agree with your proposal.

坦白地讲,我无法同意您的提案。

We're not prepared to accept your proposal at this time.

我们这一次不准备接受你们的建议。

To be quite honest, we don't believe this product will sell very well in China.

说老实话,我们不相信这种产品在中国会卖得好。

I'm afraid that won't be possible, much as we'd like to.

尽管我们很想这样做,但恐怕不行了。

——以上适合于谈判中赞同或反对对方的观点

Would you care to answer my question on the warranty?

你可以回答我有关保证的问题吗?

I don't know whether you care to answer right away.

我不知道你是否愿意立即回答。

Anything else you want to bring up for discussion.

你还有什么问题要提出来供双方讨论的吗？

By the way, before leaving this subject, I would like to add a few comments.

在结束这个问题之前顺便一提，我希望能再提出一些看法。

I would like to ask you a favor.

我可以提出一个要求吗？

We can not be sure what you want unless you tell us.

希望你能告诉我们，要不然我们无法确定你想要的是什么。

Could you please explain the premises of your argument in more detail?

你能详细说明你们的论据吗？

I have to raise some issues which may be embarrassing.

我必须提出一些比较尴尬的问题。

I'd like to know how you reached your conclusions.

我想知道你们是如何得出结论的。

Our position on the issue is very simple.

我们的意见很简单。

That's the basic problem.

这是最基本的问题。

——以上适合于在谈判中提出问题

I know I can count on you.

我知道我可以相信你。

I see what you mean.

我明白您的意思。

We are here to solve problems.

我们是来解决问题的。

We have another plan.

我们还有一个计划。

Thanks for reminding us.

谢谢你的提醒。

If you insist, I will comply with your request.

如果你坚持,我们会遵照你的要求。

Let's compromise.

让我们还是各退一步吧。

We are always willing to cooperate with you and if necessary make some concessions.

我们是愿意与你们合作的,如果可能还可以做些让步。

If you have any comment about these clauses, do not hesitate to make.

对这些条款有何意见,请尽管提,不必客气。

——以上适合于在谈判中表示有诚意促成合作

We must stress that these payment terms are very important to us.

我们必须强调这些付款条件对我们很重要。

Please be aware that this is a crucial issue to us.

请了解这一点对我们至关重要。

I don't know whether you realize it, but this condition is essential to us.

我不知道你是否了解,但是这个条件对我们是必要的。

We'd like you to consider our request once again.

我们希望贵方再次考虑我们的要求。

——以上适合于在谈判中坚守自己的条件

Are you there is some room for negotiation?

你们还有商量的余地吗?

There should always be exceptions to the rule.

凡事总有例外。

Let us imagine a hypothetical case where we disagree.

让我们假设一个我们不同意的状况。

We can work out the details next time.

我们可以下次再来解决细节问题。

I would not waste my time pursuing that.

如果是我的话，不会将时间浪费在这里。

H eW 情景对话 Situational Dialogue

Part 1

A: What is the time of negotiation?

B: They scheduled the negotiation at nine tomorrow morning.

A: Are you ready to face the negotiation?

B: We are ready.

A: How would you like to proceed with the negotiations?

B: I think we need more self-confidence and information.

A: Yes. Better have something we can get our hands on rather than just spend all our time talking. Let's prepare respective task again.

B: All right. I think we would have a famous outcome.

Part 2

A: Good morning, Mr. John.

B: Good morning, Mr. Brown.

A: I am glad to talk with you about the cooperation. I hope this meeting will be productive.

B: Yes. We will. Would anyone like something to drink before we begin?

A: No, thanks. Let's negotiate the payment of the deal.

(a moment later)

B: May I propose that we break for coffee now?

A: All right. We can think over your terms proposed by you using this period of time.

Part 3

A: Nice to meet you, Jane. Is this the first time to the states?

B: Nice to meet you, John. I have been here a few times in the past.

A: Great, so you know your way around then. But if there's any thing we can do to make your stay more comfortable, don't hesitate to ask.

B: Thank you. That's very kind of you.

A: Not at all. Now, shall we get down to business?

B: Please.

A: I think we can handle this pretty quickly. We have studied the market closely and I think we can make you a very attractive offer. We are prepared to give you $10 per unit delivered to Beijing. That's U. S. dollars of course.

B: That's a lot less than we were expecting. It's not even chose to what we were talking about over the phone.

A: I know, but there is nothing I can do.

B: But still, if we take that price, my company won't even be able to pay for my trip here.

A: Not in the long run. We can keep our cooperation relationship. When the circumstance changes we can give you a better price.

B: We're not prepared to accept your proposal at this time. If you give a rational price, we will have a consideration of the deal.

A: I'm afraid that won't be possible, much as we'd like to.

B: I really don't see where there is anything to be gained by continuing this negotiation. Let's say goodbye and part.

A: Oh. Well, I don't think things are at a stand still.

B: We are here to solve problems. I certainly hope we will draw a good conclusion.

A: Well, we can shave a little off the price we discussed over the phone.

Part 4

A: Excuse me? I have to raise some issues which may be embarrassing.

B: Yes. please!

A: I don't know whether you care to answer right away that your company's products have a low possession of market. Why you ask a so high price. Could you please explain the premises of your argument in more detail?

B: Yes. I am glad to answer this question. Because our products is innovated for a short time, broading market needs time. But low market possession doesn't indicate it's low quality.

A: We trust you. But your price is too high. Please be aware that this is a crucial issue to us.

B: We are always willing to cooperate with you and if necessary make some concessions. Let's compromise. We choose a eclectic price. All right?

A: I think the negotiations on the price turned out to be very successful.

B: We'll come out from this meeting as winners. It is a pleasure to cooperate with you.

译文

Part 1

A: 谈判是在什么时间？

B: 他们把谈判时间订在明天早上9点。

A: 你们准备好面对谈判了吗？

B: 我们准备好了。

A: 你认为该怎样来进行这次谈判呢？

B: 我想我们需要更多的自信和信息。

A: 是的。有些实际材料拿到手总比坐着闲聊强。让我们再准备一下各自的任务吧。

B: 好的。我认为我们会有个令人满意的结果的。

Part 2

A: 早上好，约翰先生。

B: 早上好，布朗先生。

A: 非常高兴能和您谈谈我们合作的问题。我希望这次谈判将会是富有成效的。

B: 是的。我们会的。在我们正式开始前，大家喝点什么吧？

A: 不了，谢谢。让我们谈谈这笔交易的付款问题吧。

（一会儿之后）

B: 我可以提议休息一下，喝杯咖啡吗？

A: 好的。我们也能利用这段时间来仔细考虑一下你们提出的条款。

Part 3

A: 很高兴见到你，珍妮。这是你第一次来美国吗？

B: 见到你很高兴，约翰。我以前来过这儿有几次了。

A: 非常好。那你对周围的环境应该熟悉了吧。如果有任何我们可以帮助的地方,请尽管开口。

B: 谢谢你。你人真好。

A: 别客气。现在我们来谈谈正事吧。

B: 请讲。

A: 我们仔细研究过市场,应该可以提供非常有吸引力的价码。
报价是 10 元,并将货送到北京。当然是指美金。

B: 这比我们预期的价格低了很多。跟我们在电话中提到的也差
很多。

A: 我知道,但我也无能为力。

B: 这种价钱,根本连到这里的差旅费都不够。

A: 从长远来看不是这样的。我们能保持我们的合作关系。情况
改变后我们就能给你一个好的价钱。

B: 我们这次不准备接受你的意见。如果你给个合理的价格,我
们会考虑一下这个问题的。

A: 恐怕这是不可能的,尽管我很希望那样。

B: 我想再谈下去也没有意义了。干脆说再见,咱们分道扬镳。

A: 哦。我想应该还有回旋的余地。

B: 我们来是解决问题的。我当然希望我们能得到一个满意
的结。

A: 电话里谈的价格,我们可以再降低一点。

Part 4

A: 请原谅。我必须提出一些比较尴尬的问题。

B: 是的。请说。

A: 我不知道是否你愿意立即回答这个问题。你们公司的市场
占有率这么低,为什么会要一个这么高的价格呢? 你能详
细说明你们的论据吗?

B: 是的。我很高兴回答这个问题。因为我们的产品研发出来
的时间很短,拓宽市场需要时间。但是低的市场占有率并

不表明它的质量低啊。

A: 我们相信你。但是你们的价格太高了。请了解这一点对我们至关重要。

B: 我们是愿意与你们合作的,如果可能还可以做些让步。让我们各让一步吧。我们选择一个折衷的价位,好吗?

A: 我认为我们就价格的谈判是成功的。

B: 这次会谈的结果将是双赢的。很高兴跟你们合作。

必备词汇　　Necessary Vocabulary

dismiss *v.* 解散,下课

go along with 赞同,附和

warranty *n.* (正当)理由,保证

premise *n.* 前提

embarrassing *adj.* 令人为难的

comply with 照做

compromise *v.* 妥协,折衷

hesitate *v.* 犹豫,踌躇

low quality 低质量

eclectic *adj.* 兼收并蓄的;折衷的

Contract 合同

　　合同是合作双方的契约性规定,具有法律效应,在签订合同时一定要弄清楚有关合同的各项条款,稍有疏忽就可能承受意外的损失。

eHow 基本句型 Sentence Patterns

We have to discuss about. . .

我们不得不讨论一下……

When will the contract be ready?

合同何时准备好？

Do you think there is something wrong with. . .

你认为关于……还有问题吗？

When shall we sign the contract?

我们什么时候签合同呢？

Here are the two originals of the contract we prepared.

这是我们准备好的两份合同正本。

eHow 星级典句 Classical Sentences

I still have some questions concerning our contract.

就合同方面我还有些问题要问。

Do you think there is something wrong with the contract?

你认为合同有问题吗？

We'd like to clear up some points connected with the technical part of the contract.

我们希望搞清楚有关合同中技术方面的几个问题。

We'll have to discuss about the total contract price.

我们不得不讨论一下合同的总价格问题。

Do you have any comment on this clause.

你对这一条款有何看法？

——以上适合于就合同问题进行提问

Don't you think it necessary to have a close study of the contract to avoid anything missing?

你不觉得应该仔细检查一下合同,以免遗漏什么吗?

We have agreed on all terms in the contract. Shall we sign it next week?

我们对合同各项条款全无异议,下周签合同如何?

Would you please read the draft contract and make your moments about the terms?

请仔细阅读合同草案,并就合同各条款提出你的看法好吗?

If you have any comment about these clauses, do not hesitate to make.

对这些条款有何意见,请尽管提,不必客气。

——以上适合于就合同问题征询对方意见

We are really glad to see you so constructive in helping settle the problems as regards the signing of the contract.

我们很高兴您在解决有关合同的问题上如此具有建设性。

The negotiations on the rights and obligations of the parties under contract turned out to be very successful.

就合同双方权利与义务方面的谈判非常成功。

We don't have any different opinions about the contractual obligations of both parties.

就合同双方要承担的义务方面,我们没有什么意见。

The two parties involved in a contract have the obligation to execute the contract.

合同双方有义务履行合同。

We hope that the next negotiation will be the last one before signing the contract.

我们希望下一轮谈判将是签订合同前的最后一轮谈判。

We are prepared to reconsider amending the contract.

我们可以重新考虑修改合同。

The contract will be sent to you by air mail for your signature.

合同会航邮给你签字。

——以上适合于表示签订合同进展顺利

We'd like you to consider our request once again.

我们希望贵方再次考虑我们的要求。

We can't agree with the alterations and amendments to the contract.

我们无法同意对合同的变动和修改。

That's international practice. We can't break it.

这是国际惯例,我们不能违背。

——以上适合于表示坚持更改合同或是维持原来条款

情景对话 Situational Dialogue

Part 1

A: Let's go on our negotiation about the contract. And I hope that this negotiation will be the last one before signing the contract.

B: I still have some questions concerning our contract.

A: If you have any comment about these clauses, do not hesitate to make. Please!

B: Thank you. I think we should add one term that we should set up a mechanism of punishment so that both sides can carry on his duty rightly.

A: We are really glad to see you so constructive in helping settle the problems as regards the signing of the contract. We completely agree with your opinion.

B: Thank you very much.

A: I think the negotiations on the rights and obligations of the parties under contract turned out to be very successful.

B: Yes. We have agreed on all terms in the contract. Shall we sign it next week?

A: All right. Next Monday is OK?

B: Yes. It's a pleasure to cooperate with you.

A: Me too.

Part 2

A: We have to discuss about payment in the contract.

B: Do you have any comment on this clause?

A: Yes. I think the expenses of shipment should be paid by you.

B: What? Are you joking? The expenses should be paid by purchaser. That's international practice. We can't break it.

A: But your price of the goods is too high. If you won't decline the price of products, you should pay the expenses of shipment.

B: We can't agree with the alterations and amendments to the contract.

A: We'd like you to consider our request once again. We are single-hearted but you no.

B: We should have a break and I think we should think it over.

A: All right.

译文

Part 1

A: 让我们继续关于合同的讨论吧。我希望这次谈判是签订合同之前的最后一次谈判了。

B: 关于这个合同我还有一些问题要问。

A: 对这些条款有何意见,请尽管提,不必客气。请说!

B: 谢谢你。我认为我们应该增加一个条款,那就是我们应该建立一种惩罚机制以便双方能更好地履行自己的义务。

A: 我们很高兴您在解决有关合同的问题上如此具有建设性。我们完全同意您的建议。

B: 非常感谢。

A: 我认为就合同双方的权利与义务方面的谈判非常成功。

B: 是的。我们对合同各项条款达成一致,下周签合同如何?

A: 好的。下周一怎么样?

B: 好。跟你们合作真是很愉快。

A: 我也是。

Part 2

A: 我们得讨论一下合同中的付款问题。

B: 你对这一条款有何看法?

A: 是的。我认为货运的费用应该由你方来出。

B: 什么?你是在开玩笑吗?货运的费用应该由买方来出,这是国际惯例,我们不能违背。

A: 但是你们货物的价格太高。如果你们不降低产品的价格,你们就应该偿付货运的费用。

B: 我们无法同意对合同的变动和修改。

A: 我们希望贵方再次考虑我们的要求。我们是有诚意的但是你们没有。

获悉我方提供的货物给你方带来了麻烦,我们感到十分抱歉。

Please return at our expense the goods you have received.

请将所收货物退回,运费由我方支付。

I'm very sorry for any unnecessary hardship you had suffered.

对你方所承受的不必要的损失,我方深表抱歉。

The mistake is on our end and we will take care of it. I'll arrange a special delivery so that you'll have them by tomorrow.

这次是我们的失误,我们会注意的。我会安排一个快递,这样的话明天你们就能收到它们。

I'm sorry but I'll check it and call you back as soon as possible.

很抱歉,但是我会检查一下并尽快给您回电话的。

How can we best deal with this problem to your satisfaction?

我们应该怎样处理这个问题你们才能满意呢?

——以上适合于卖方表示愿意承担责任

I'd like to make a careful inquiry into the damage once again to make sure of it.

为弄清楚事实,我会对此次破损的情况再做仔细的检查。

I'll give the matter a thorough investigation before we come to a final solution.

在最后解决问题之前,我会再认真调查此事的。

I'll check into it again to find out what really happened.

我会再检查一下,看看究竟发生了什么。

——以上适合于买卖双方在做出结论前的仔细调查

We consider this matter closed.

我们希望此事到此为止。

The claim was turned down.

我方拒绝索赔。

For the claim is without foundations, it can't be accepted.

因为没有任何根据,此项索赔不能被接受。

Without sufficient evidence to support your claim it is untenable, and we can see no point in pursuing it further.

没有充分的证据,你方索赔是站不住脚的,继续纠缠此事毫无意义。

——以上适合于卖方拒绝索赔

H W 情景对话 Situational Dialogue

Part 1

A: Good morning, Mr. John. I'm sorry to have you here in such a busy season.

B: Never mind.

A: If you don't mind, I will get down straight to the actual business.

B: All right.

A: However reluctant we are, we have to make the following complaint that the quality of products last time we have ordered is not satisfied to our customers. This defect is threatening the loss of our best customers.

B: I am sorry to hear that and we fully understand your position at this moment. I'll give the matter a thorough investigation before we come to a final solution.

A: As we have a very good beginning of business between us we believe you will give us a satisfactory answer.

B: From our previous transactions you realize that this sort of problem is quite unusual.

A: Yes. I believe in that.

B: Thank you for the chance. If we draw a conclusion, I will call you as soon as possible.

A: Thank you.

Part 2

A: I know the making of complaint is an unpleasant business in the practice of foreign trade, but I very much regret to inform you that there are some problems with your products.

B: What?

A: On unwrapping the cases, we found there are lots of porcelain bottle cracked. As the trouble there from is so serious, we have to lodge a claim against you.

B: We have shipping documents to prove that the good were received by the carrier in perfect condition. Therefore, they must have been damaged in route.

A: What you have said is irrational, and we think you should compensate for all the loss.

B: As the damage is apparently due to rough handling in transit, it is appropriate for you to file your claim with the relevant insurance company.

A: With a view to our long business relations we hope we can handle the problem folksy. But if you keep this opinion, we think we must go to the courtroom.

B: We consider this matter closed. For the claim is without foundations, it can't be accepted. We will wait you at the courtroom.

伶牙俐齿 英语口语

Part 3

A: To the great dissatisfaction of our customers, the quality of your first shipment is not in conformity with the specifications.

B: I am sorry to hear that you have trouble with the goods we supplied. And we appreciate your bringing this matter to our attention.

A: Thank you for your comprehension.

B: I'll check into it again to find out what really happened. And we will compensate the loss arose by our bad quality.

A: Thank you very much. It is a pleasure to cooperate with you.

译文

Part 1

A: 早上好,约翰先生。很抱歉在生意繁忙的时候把您请到这里来。

B: 没有关系。

A: 如果您不介意,我们还是直奔主题吧。

B: 好的。

A: 虽然极不愿意,但我方不得不提出以下抱怨,我们上次订货的质量不能使我们的客户满意。这个缺点可能会使我们面临失去最好的客户的威胁。

B: 听到这个我很抱歉,我们完全理解你方此刻的处境。在最后解决问题之前,我会再认真调查此事的。

A: 由于我们之间有着良好的业务开端,我相信您能给我们一个满意的答复。

B: 从我们双方以往的交易中您应当了解,这次事件纯属偶然。

A: 是的。我相信。

B: 谢谢您给的机会。如果我得出结论,我会尽快打电话给您的。

A: 谢谢。

220

Part 2

A: 我明白在外贸业务中提出抱怨是件令人不愉快的事,但是我很遗憾地告诉你,你们的产品有些问题。

B: 什么?

A: 打开箱子我们发现许多瓷瓶都破裂了。由此引起的麻烦太严重,我方不得不向你方提出索赔。

B: 我们有装运单证明,承运人在收货时货是完整无损的。因此,货物是在运输途中损坏的。

A: 你说的根本没有道理,我们认为你方应该赔偿我们全部损失。

B: 货物的损坏明显是由运输途中的粗暴搬运造成的,请你向相关保险公司索赔。

A: 考虑到我们长期的业务关系,我们希望我们能和气地处理这个问题。但是如果你们保持这个态度,我想我们必须在法庭上解决了。

B: 我想此事到此为止。你们的索赔毫无根据,不能被接受。我们会在法庭上等你们的。

Part 3

A: 令我方顾客十分不满意的是,你方第一批货物的质量与规定不符。

B: 获悉我方提供的货物给你方带来麻烦,我们感到十分抱歉。并且我们非常感谢贵公司提醒我们注意此事。

A: 谢谢你们的理解。

B: 我会再检查一下,看看究竟发生了什么。并且我们会赔偿由于我们低质量产品所带给你们的损失。

A: 非常感谢。跟你们合作很愉快。

必备词汇　Necessary Vocabulary

complaint *n.* 投诉,抱怨

claim *n.* 要求,索要

unwrap *v.* 打开,展开

dissatisfaction *n.* 不满,不平

reluctant *adj.* 勉强的

with a view to 考虑到,着眼于

investigation *n.* 调查,研究

untenable *adj.* 站不住脚的,防守不住的

satisfactory *adj.* 满意的

porcelain *adj.* 瓷制的

apparently *adv.* 显然地

folksy *adj.* 和气的,友好的

Marketing 市场营销

市场营销是商务活动的重要环节，是关于公司产品的整个策略过程，包括包装、广告、宣传、命名、销售、品牌的建立等等。

eHow 基本句型　Sentence Patterns

Our market investigation reveals that. . .

我们的市场调研显示……

According to our marketing research information, customers are particularly interested in. . .

从市场调研的信息看,客户尤其对……感兴趣。

Our targeting specific audiences are. . .

我们的目标顾客是……

Our new radio has many features. Among them is. . .

我们的新型收音机具有很多特色。其中之一就是……

I'm sure that the. . . represents a significant market opportunity for. . .

对于……来说……肯定能为他们带来莫大的市场机遇。

eHow 星级典句　Classical Sentences

When we launch a new product, we must bring customers' attention to it. If we are competing with well-known products, we should start with low prices.

当我们将新产品投入市场时,必须让消费者注意到它。如果是同名牌产品竞争,刚开始时应实施低价政策。

This could be a great marketing opportunity.

这应该是个很好的市场营销机会。

I need some suggestions on how to market my product.

我需要一些有关如何销售我公司产品的建议。

——以上适合于讨论市场营销策略

Have you thought about advertising in newspapers and magazines?

你想过在报纸和杂志上登广告吗?

We will hold three discrete marketing campaigns.

我们将会举行三次不同的营销活动。

We'll have to run a good advertising campaign.

我们得开展一场强大的广告攻势。

We will give our new product a unique name in order to build brand awareness.

我们产品的命名将独特而新颖,以树立品牌意识。

——以上适合于产品宣传、树立品牌

It's our rock bottom price.

我们的价钱是最低了。

Our product is really competitive in the world market.

我们的产品在国际市场上很有竞争力。

All in all, quality is our biggest concern.

总而言之,质量是我们最关心的。

I'm pleased to tell you all that we have found many outlets for our new products.

很高兴地告诉大家,我们已为新产品找到许多销售渠道。

I think you ought to bear in mind our costs.

我想你们应该把我们的成本考虑进去。

We have gained a market share of 20%.

我们获得了20%的市场份额。

——以上适合于向别人推销自己的产品

eH w 情景对话　Situational Dialogue

Part 1

A: Hello, Mr. John.

B: Hello, Miss. Jane.

A: I come to consult with you about that I need some suggestions on how to market my new product.

B: Oh. Do you have any datum to show me?

A: Yes. Here is the marketing research.

B: When you launch a new product, you must bring customers' attention to it. If you are competing with well-known products, you should start with low prices.

A: I agree with you. Do we need some propaganda?

B: Certainly. You should have to run a good advertising campaign so that you can build up your brand.

A: Should we advertise in newspapers or magazines?

B: It depends on your targeting specific audiences and your outlay put in the advertisement.

A: That sounds rational. Every media has itself characteristic. I think we'd better choose the radio, because our targeting specific audiences are older.

B: Yes. I think your choose will be right.

A: Thank you for your help.

B: It's my pleasure.

Part 2

A: Hello. I'm interested in your products.

B: Thank you for your inquiry. Our new radio has many features. Among them is the agility.

A: According to our marketing research information, customers are particularly interested in quality. How is your radio's quality?

B: Our product is really competitive in the world market. Its life can last more than 10 years and it is a electricity saving style. All in all, quality is our biggest concern.

A: That sounds wonderful.

B: I'm sure that this kind of radio will bring you a significant market opportunity.

A: I hope so.

译文

Part 1

A: 你好,约翰先生。

B: 你好,珍妮小姐。

A: 我来是想向您咨询一下,我需要一些有关如何销售我公司产品的建议。

B: 哦。你有什么材料让我看一下吗?

A: 是的。这是市场调研情况。

B: 当你们将新产品投入市场时,必须让消费者注意到它。如果是同名牌产品竞争,刚开始时应实施低价政策。

A: 我同意您的看法。我们需要一些宣传吗?

B: 当然了。你们需要开展一次大的广告攻势以建立你们的品牌。

A: 我们应该在报纸还是杂志上登广告?

B: 那要看你们的目标顾客和在广告上要投入的经费了。

A: 听起来很有道理。每种媒体都有它自身的特性。我想我们最好选择收音机,因为我们的目标顾客是老年人。

B: 是的。我想你们的选择会是正确的。

A: 谢谢你的帮助。

B: 我很荣幸。

Part 2

A: 你好。我对你们的产品感兴趣。

B: 谢谢您的询价。我们的收音机有很多特性,其中之一就是其灵活性。

A: 从市场调研的信息看,客户尤其对产品质量感兴趣。你们收音机的质量怎么样?

B: 我们的产品在国际市场上很有竞争力。它的寿命能持续十年以上并且很省电。总而言之,质量是我们最关心的问题。

A: 听起来真是很好啊。

B: 我确信这种收音机将会带给你们重要的市场机会。

A: 我希望是那样。

必备词汇 **Necessary Vocabulary**

investigation *n.* 调查,研究

specific *n.* 明确的,特定的

discrete *adj.* 不连续的,不同的

consult with 协商,商量

propaganda *n.* 宣传

build up 树立,增进,增大

outlay *n.* 费用

Agent 代理

代理一种好的产品能够为公司带来很高的效益，而生产商要扩大自己的市场销售渠道也离不开代理商的支持，代理商与厂商之间的相互有效沟通对双方是一种双赢的行为。

H w 基本句型　Sentence Patterns

We appreciate your efforts in pushing the sale of...

非常感激你方为推销我方……而做出的努力。

We feel sure that as our sole agent in... you are going to make a very profitable business.

作为我方在……的独家代理，我们确定你能获得非常丰厚的利润回报。

I want to sign a sole agency agreement with you on...

我想就……跟你签订一份独家代理协议。

I wish to act as an agent for...

我愿意为……做代理。

H w 星级典句　Classical Sentences

We have to insist that our agents do business on our behalf according to our terms and obtain a certain commission from their sales.

我们得坚持的是代理人必须按我方规定的条件代表我方组织成交，并收取一定的佣金。

The agent agrees to represent no other firm in the same line of business while our sole agency remains in force.

代理商在协议有效期内不代理其他公司经营的同类产品。

No special terms, rebate, discount, or commission contrary to our trade terms and quotations can be given to buyers without our permission.

未经我方许可不得给与买方不符合我方贸易条款和报价的特殊条款、回扣、折扣或佣金。

We have well established channels of distribution.

我们有良好的销售渠道。

We have decided to make you our sole agency for our products.

我们决定聘你为我们产品的独家代理。

You need to appoint an agent to push the sales.

你需要一名代理商来促销。

eHow 情景对话 Situational Dialogue

A: I want to sign a sole agency agreement with you for a period of 3 years.

B: I am interested in that. And thank you for your offer to be our sole agent and we would like to have some information about your plans for promoting the sale of our products.

A: Here is our plan. And we have done a research of our market. I think we would broad the market successfully.

B: But I think it is still too early for us to find an agent for your market.

A: No, no, no. Other manufacturer has entered the market, and if you launch you products later, I think, you will be uncompetitive.

B: I can't give you the thumbs up right now. But I will go back to consult with our directorate.

A: Thank you. I am looking forward to your favorable reply.

译文

A: 我想和你们签订一份三年的独家代理协议。

B: 我对这很感兴趣。并且谢谢你想做我们独家代理的请求,另外我们想了解你们对我们公司产品的促销计划。

A: 这是我们的计划书,并且我们已经做了一个市场调查。我想我们会成功地拓宽市场的。

B: 但是我认为在贵国市场找代理人还是为时过早的。

A: 不,不,不。其他厂商已经进入我们市场,如果您晚点投放您的产品,我想,您是缺乏竞争力的。

B: 我现在无法立刻同意你的请求。不过我会回去和我们的董事会商量的。

A: 谢谢您。那我静候佳音。

必备词汇　Necessary Vocabulary

profitable *adj.* 有利可图的

sole agency 独家经营,独家代理

behalf *n.* 利益

rebate *n.* 回扣,折扣

uncompetitive *adj.* 无竞争力的

directorate *n.* 董事会,高级职员会

Index

a couple of 两个,几个

abundant *adj.* 丰富的,充裕的

accommodation *n.* 住宿,预定铺位

accountant *n.* 会计师,会计员

adulterate *v.* 掺和,掺假

agenda *n.* 议事单,议程表

air freight 空运发货

alphabetically *adv.* 按字母顺序地

amendment *n.* 改善,改正

annual *n.* 一年一次的,每年的

apology *n.* 道歉

apparently *adv.* 显然地

appoint *v.* 指定,任命,委任

appointment *n.* 约会,指定

appreciate *v.* 赏识,感激

as luck would have it 碰巧

available *adj.* 可用到的,可利用的

bachelor *n.* 学士

banquet *n.* 宴会

be it so 就这样吧,好吧

behalf *n.* 利益

bonus *n.* 奖金,红利

book up 预定

brash *adj.* 仓促的,性急的

brochure *n.* 小册子

build up 树立,增进,增大

business *n.* 生意,贸易,营业,买卖

capacity *n.* 容量,生产量

capital *adj.* 大写的

catalogue *n.* 目录

certification *n.* 证明

chary *adj.* 仔细的,谨慎的

check-in *n.* 报到处,登记处

check-out *n.* 付账离开,结账

cheque *n.* 支票

chopstick *n.* 筷子

cinema *n.* 电影院

circumspect *adj.* 周到的,慎重的

claim *n.* 要求,索要

clause *n.* 条款

clear up 整理,澄清

clumsy *adj.* 笨拙的

comment on 评论

competitive *adj.* 竞争的

complaint *n.* 投诉,抱怨

complementarity *n.* 补充

compliment *n.* 称赞,赞扬

comply with 照做

compromise *n.* 妥协,折衷

compromise *v.* 妥协,折衷

concession *n.* 让步

conclude *v.* 决定,做出结论

concretely *adv.* 具体地

congratulations *n.* 祝贺

constructive *adj.* 建设性的

consult with 协商, 商量

consume *v.* 消耗, 消费

contract *n.* 合同, 契约

contractual *adj.* 契约的

convenient *adj.* 方便的

cooperation *n.* 合作, 协作

countryside *n.* 乡下

credit *n.* 信用, 银行存款

credit *v.* 把……归功于……, 信任

crowded *adj.* 拥挤的, 塞满的

customs declaration form 通关申报表格

declare *v.* (向海关)申报进口应纳税之货物

declining *adj.* 倾斜的, 衰退中的

deduct from *v.* 扣除

delay *v.* 耽搁

delicious *adj.* 美味的

delivery *n.* 递送, 交付

departure *n.* 启程, 出发, 离开

depict *v.* 描述, 叙述

deposit *v.* 存款, 存放物

deserve *v.* 应受, 值得

dessert *n.* 甜品, 点心

detailed *adj.* 详细的, 逐条的

directorate *n.* 董事会, 高级职员会

discharge *v.* 卸下, 放出

discount *n.* 折扣

discrete *adj.* 不连续的, 不同的

dismiss *v.* 解散, 下课

disposal *n.* 安排,处理

dissatisfaction *n.* 不满,不平

door-to-door 挨户访问的

double room *n.* 双人房

draft *v.* 起草,草拟

drop a line 写信给某人

eclectic *adj.* 兼收并蓄的,折衷的

effective *adj.* 有效的

electrograph *n.* 传真机

electronic *adj.* 电子的

embarrassing *adj.* 令人为难的

employee *n.* 职工,雇员

enjoyable *adj.* 令人愉快的,可享受的

entertainment *n.* 娱乐

equipment *n.* 装备,设备

essential *adj.* 基本的,必要的

excellent *adj.* 卓越的,极好的

exception *n.* 除外,例外

execution *n.* 实行,执行

exhibit *n.* 展览品,陈列品

extremely *adv.* 极其地

facilitate *v.* 使容易,使便利

fair price 公平价格

famed *n.* 闻名的,著名的

fantastic *adj.* 妙极了

fashionable *adj.* 流行的,时髦的

favorable *adj.* 良好的,讨人喜欢的

favorite *n.* 特别喜欢的人或事物

fellow *n.* 伙伴

fiction *n.* 小说，虚构

finely *adv.* 美好地，细微地

first-class *n.* 头等舱

five-star *adj.* 五星的，最高级的

flatter *v.* 过分夸奖，奉承

flight *n.* 飞机的航班

fog *n.* 雾，烟雾，尘雾

folksy *adj.* 和气的，友好的

fuzzy *adj.* 模糊的，失真的

general *adj.* 一般的，普通的

general manager 总经理

get down to 开始认真考虑

go along with 赞同，附和

grateful *adj.* 感激的，感谢的

gratifying *adj.* 悦人的，令人满足的

gratitude *n.* 感谢，感激

greenback *n.* 美钞，背部为绿色之动物

guarantee *n.* 保证，保证书，担保

gym *n.* 体育，体育馆，体操

handle *v.* 处理，运用

hang on to 紧紧握住

have a pleasant journey 一路顺风，一路平安

have sth. at one's fingers 精通某事物

hectare *n.* 公顷

helmet *n.* 头盔，钢盔

hesitate *v.* 犹豫，踌躇

hobby *n.* 业余爱好

honoured *adj.* 荣幸的

illustration *n.* 例子，图表

immigration *n.* 移居入境,外来的移民

impressive *adj.* 给人深刻印象的

in accordance with 与……一致,依照

in advance 预先,提前

in charge of 负责,照顾,经营

in range of 在……范围之内

in short 简言之

inconvenient *adj.* 不便的,有困难的

indebted *adj.* 负债的,感恩的

indicator *n.* 指示器

innovation *n.* 改革,创新

inquiry *n.* 咨询,调查

introduce *v.* 介绍

investigation *n.* 调查,研究

jam *v.* 堵塞,塞满

journey *n.* 旅行,旅程

laundry *n.* 要洗的衣服,洗衣店

layout *n.* 规划,布局

lobby *n.* 大厅,休息室

logical *adj.* 合理的

look forward to 期待,盼望

look up 拜访,尊敬

low quality 低质量

mail-cart *n.* 邮车

manufacture *v.* 制造,加工

margin *n.* 利润

maximum *n.* 最大量,最大限度

mechanism *n.* 机制

minimum price 最低价

motel *n.* 汽车旅馆

mutual benefit 互惠,互利

negotiation *n.* 商议,谈判

newcomer *n.* 新到的人,新来的人

nonstop *adj.* 不断的

obligation *n.* 义务,职责

occasional *adj.* 偶然的,临时的

Olympiad *n.* 奥林匹克运动会

on grounds of 根据

on the high side (价格)偏高

one-up *n.* 领先的,占上风的

original *n.* 原物,原件

outlay *n.* 费用

overdue *adj.* 过期的,迟到的

overlook *v.* 忽视

owing to 由于,因……之缘故

par value *n.* 票面价值,面值

parcel *n.* 包裹

partial *adj.* 部分的,局部的

pattern *n.* 样品,图样

payable *adj.* 可付的,应付的

penalty *n.* 处罚,罚款

period of validity 有效期

personal *adj.* 私人的,个人的,针对个人的

personally *adv.* 亲自

pick-up *n.* 提取,搭便车

porcelain *adj.* 瓷制的

postage *n.* 邮资

postage paid 邮资已付

postpone *v.* 推迟,延迟

precedent *n.* 先例

precisian *n.* 严谨的人,严格遵守规则的人

premise *n.* 前提

presentation *n.* 表现,表达

profitable *adj.* 有利可图的

profound *adj.* 深刻的,意义深远的

propaganda *n.* 宣传

proposal *n.* 提议,建议

publicity *n.* 公开

punctual *adj.* 严守时刻的,准时的

put a premium 奖励

put off 推迟,拖延

put through 接通

quote *v.* 引用,引证

rate *n.* 价格,费用

raw *adj.* 未加工的

rear *adj.* 后面的,背面的

rebate *n.* 回扣,折扣

receipt *n.* 收条,收据

reception *n.* 接待,招待

reconsider *v.* 重新考虑,重新审议

region *n.* 地方,区域

register *v.* 登记,注册,挂号

regrettable *adj.* 可叹的,可惜的

relaxation *n.* 放松

relevant *adj.* 有关的,相应的

reluctant *adj.* 勉强的

remittance *n.* 汇款,汇寄之款

reopen *v.* 重开,再开始

representative *n. / adj.* 代表;典型的,有代表性的

reputation *n.* 名誉,名声

reservation *n.* 保留,预定,预约

reserve *v.* 预定,预约

restaurant *n.* 餐馆,饭店

retail price 零售价

run out 被用完

salon *n.* 沙龙

sample *n.* 样品,标本,例子

satisfactory *adj.* 满意的

savings account 储蓄存款账户

schedule *n.* 时间表,进度表

see off 送行

shipment *n.* 装船,出货

showroom *n.* (商品、样品的)陈列室

sight-seeing *n.* 观光,游览

simplify *v.* 简单化,单一化

sincerely *adv.* 真诚地

sincerity *n.* 诚挚,真诚

single-hearted *adj.* 有诚意的

sip *v.* 呷吸

so as to 使得,以致

sole agency 独家经营,独家代理

solicitor *n.* 律师,法律顾问

soup *n.* 汤

special discount 特别折扣

specialize *v.* 专攻,专门研究

specialize in 擅长于,专攻

specific *n.* 明确的,特定的

splendid *adj.* 壮丽的,辉煌的

split *v.* 分裂,分离

sprinkle *v.* 洒,喷洒

stand *n.* 台,看台,架子

standard *adj.* 标准的,权威的,第一流的

staple *v.* 装订

stipulation *n.* 约定,约束,契约

strenuous *adj.* 紧张的,尽心发奋的

stressful *adj.* 产生压力的,使紧迫的

symbolize *v.* 象征

tag *n.* 标签,标记符

take charge 看管,负责

take into consideration 考虑到

take off *v.* 起飞

tax-free *adj.* 免税的,无税的

terminus *n.* 终点站,终点

textile *n.* 纺织品

Tibet *n.* 西藏

tie up 占用,密切联系,合伙

top priority 应予最优先考虑的事

traffic jam 交通堵塞

transaction *v.* 交易,事务

transfer *n.* 传递,转移

tranship *v.* 换船,换车

trivial *adj.* 琐碎的

turbulence *n.* 颠簸,动荡

uncompetitive *adj.* 无竞争力的

undeliverable *adj.* 无法投递的,无法送达的

unfortunately *adv.* 不幸地

unilateral *adj.* 单方面的,单边的

unit cost 单价,单位成本

untenable *adj.* 站不住脚的,防守不住的

unwrap *v.* 打开,展开

urgent *adj.* 急迫的,紧急的

urgent need 急需的

valid *adj.* 有效的,有根据的

validity *n.* 有效性,合法性,正确性

vice 代理,副的

volume *n.* 量

warehouse *n.* 仓库,货栈

warranty *n.* （正当）理由,保证

washcloth *n.* 毛巾,面巾

wise *adj.* 明智的,聪明的

with a view to 考虑到,着眼于

with open arms 热情地,友好地

withdraw *v.* 收回,撤出

wonderful *adj.* 令人惊奇的,极好的

yup *int.* 是,是的